MURDER IN THE
THIRD ACT

A 1920S HISTORICAL COZY MYSTERY (AN EVIE
PARKER MYSTERY BOOK 6)

SONIA PARIN

ISBN: 9781697766141

CHAPTER 1

Wilfred Hartigan – Publisher
Mrs. Virginia Otway-Wells (Toodles) – Evie's
grandmother

Summer 1920
Halton House, Berkshire

"*I* am going to pay dearly for this," Evie
whispered under her breath. Taking her aim,
she pictured the croquet ball flying through the hoop. A
part of her urged her to miss the shot and allow her
esteemed guest to win.

A dozen voices chorused in the back of her mind.

Yes, let him win.

Out of the corner of her eye, Evie saw the dowagers,

Henrietta and Sara, sitting under the shade of an oak tree and her granny, Toodles, sitting between them. They smiled and nodded as they carried on their murmured conversation. They were, no doubt, discussing the merits of Evie letting her opponent win.

Wilfred Hartigan had been at Halton House for two days. Every time Evie had come within hearing of the dowagers and her granny, they had been talking of no one else. It had been Wilfred this and Wilfred that. His broad shoulders had received the utmost attention, as had his perfect profile, patrician nose, firm yet inviting lips, not to mention his sparkling blue eyes. Oh, and the rich mahogany shade of his locks. Every inch of the man had come under scrutiny and every other remark she'd over-heard had questioned Evie's lack of interest in the man.

What did they expect her to do? She had a house full of guests as well as her granny to entertain. Although, clearly, Toodles could find her own entertainment.

Straightening, Evie huffed out a breath and mentally argued with her inner peanut gallery. Honestly, if she couldn't play to win, then she didn't see the point of both-ering to play a game at all.

Her guest, Wilfred Hartigan, swung his mallet and rested it on his shoulder, a confident smile sparkling right back at her.

"Are you waiting for the wind to change direction?" Tom Winchester, her bodyguard who had come to work for her under the guise of chauffeuring her around and now lived on the outskirts of the estate, asked.

Evie huffed again and blew a lock of hair out of her eye. "If you must know, I am strategizing." Should she miss? And by how much? Could she come close to missing? Could she miss and still maintain a level of competency? Evie pushed the thoughts aside and scooped in a breath. "This one is for all the women who think they should let a man win," she whispered. Taking her position again, Evie curled her fingers around the mallet and gave the ball a light tap. At least, that had been her intention.

The ball lifted off the ground, flew across the lawn, missed the hoop and collided with full force against Wilfred Hartigan's knee.

With a yelp, he crumbled to the ground, holding his leg as he groaned, "I yield. I yield."

Evie glanced over her shoulder in time to see her granny, Toodles, rolling her eyes, the dowager, Henrietta, holding a handkerchief against her chest and Sara, her mother-in-law, pressing her hands to her cheeks, her eyes bright with astonishment.

"I am so sorry, Wilfred," Evie exclaimed and hurried to his side. "Are you quite all right or should I call for a doctor?"

"Oh, no, my lady. You needn't bother. I'm sure the agonizing pain will soon subside."

"Evie," she said. "I insist you call me Evie."

Wilfred raised a hand as if to shield himself from further injury. "Yes, of course, Evie." Grimacing, he curled up into a tight ball.

Evie had the distinct impression he wished to roll around the lawn but was, in fact, employing the utmost control to regain a modicum of male dignity and doing his best to straighten.

Turning slightly, she gestured to Tom and mouthed, "Help him."

Tom shrugged.

Yes, indeed. What could he do?

She supposed it could have been worse...

"Would you like some tea?" she offered.

Wilfred Hartigan's face scrunched up and paled, matching the pristine white of Evie's gown. He now looked utterly horrified.

It seemed the offer of tea had caused him more pain than a croquet ball hitting his knee.

Tom approached, crouched down and handed Wilfred Hartigan a small silver flask.

Looking at it, Wilfred hesitated.

"Oh, do go on. I'm sure the others won't mind," Evie encouraged.

Nodding, he took the flask and downed the contents in greedy gulps. Returning the empty flask, he said, "I think perhaps I should refrain from further participating in any competitive activities."

Oh, but he had looked so confident standing there with his mallet and his brilliant smile. Honestly, if she lived to be one hundred, she would still fail to gain any insightful understanding of the male species.

At a nod from Wilfred, Tom clasped his hand around his arm and helped him up.

"If you need us, we'll be in the library," Tom said and headed back inside with Wilfred hobbling beside him.

Evie turned and saw her other guests reaching the crest in the hill as they returned from their walk around the park. Thinking it would take them a good fifteen minutes to walk all the way back, Evie strolled toward the dowagers and sat down.

Henrietta patted her hand. "Evangeline, you mustn't fret."

"I had no intention of fretting. That was nothing but an accident."

The dowagers exchanged a look and Evie noticed her granny joining in the silent conversation.

Since her much anticipated arrival, Toodles had surprised Evie by settling in as if she were at home. Not a single word of complaint had passed her lips. Instead, she had praised everything from her accommodation to the weather. It had surprised Evie because she had been expecting her granny to launch an offensive assault in an effort to dissuade Evie from making England her permanent home. Then again, when Toodles wanted something, she employed any means possible to get it and that could involve underhanded means. Evie suspected she had yet to see her granny's best efforts at work and she would no doubt deploy them when Evie least expected her to.

Lifting her chin, Evie said, "Whatever is on your minds, I would appreciate it if you would all please spare me the details."

Henrietta pursed her lips.

Toodles took a sip of her lemonade and gave her the sweetest smile she reserved for her amusing remarks. "What more can we expect, I wonder? The man has been here two days. You have already nearly run him over with your roadster…"

"An accident," Evie murmured. "And, it's not my roadster. It belongs to Tom."

"Then you scalded the poor man with your hot tea," Toodles continued. "I've never known you to have butter fingers."

"My finger twitched." The day before, when she had admittedly nearly ended Wilfred's life, she had been

5

taking driving lessons from Tom and had been holding onto the steering wheel so hard her fingers had ached for the rest of the day. Even holding a teacup had been a trial.

"Anyone would think you have an aversion to the man," Sara exclaimed, "but we know that to be false because you invited him here yourself."

"At your behest," Evie murmured.

"As I recall, you asked me to provide you with a list of interesting men," Sara said. "Wilfred Hartigan happens to be one of them. He single-handedly resuscitated the publishing house he inherited from his grandfather. Visit anyone's library and you will find a Hartigan Imprint book on the shelves. Dig around enough and you will also find one of his popular trashy novels hidden behind a cushion." Sara reached for a cucumber sandwich and sat back to nibble on it. "If you are not interested in the man, you only needed to say so. At the rate you are going, my dear Evie, you will become a prime suspect in one of your murder cases."

Despite being deep in conversation with Henrietta, Toodles heard every word Sara had said. "Excuse me a moment, Henrietta." She leaned forward. "Murder?"

"We're discussing books, Granny," Evie said. "Nothing to worry about."

Toodles laughed. "Birdie, you can pull the wool over your mother's eyes but this is me you're talking to."

"Birdie?" Henrietta asked.

"It's… It's my granny's pet name for me."

Toodles smiled. "As a child, she could never sit still for longer than a minute. It drove her nanny mad. In the end, we had to retire Nanny Stevens to a cottage on the estate. The poor woman's nerves were frail from all the running around she did. I always say, if you are going to be around children, you must have a strong constitution. Anyhow, Evie always made me think of little birds constantly hoping around and flying from tree to tree."

It took a moment for Henrietta to digest the explanation. "I see." She turned to Evie. "I hope you don't expect me to adopt the sobriquet. I'm rather fond of calling you Evangeline."

Evie patted her hand. "That's perfectly fine, Henrietta. I rather like knowing there is at least one person happy to use my full name. I always felt being called Birdie made me sound flighty and... well, not altogether here."

"Oh, I would never say that about you, my dear." Henrietta turned to Toodles. "Your granddaughter has displayed impressive skills in the art of detecting."

"Detecting what?" Toodles asked, her voice devoid of any expression.

Henrietta loaded her reply with mirth. "Why, killers, of course."

Her granny's eyebrows curved upward. "Why am I only hearing about this now?"

Evie gave a small shrug. "It's hardly a suitable topic."

"Really?" Henrietta exclaimed. "I seem to recall being entertained over dinner with the liveliest conversation about one mysterious death or another."

Toodles straightened in her chair. "Well, I aim to hear more about your detecting adventures..."

Meaning, she would get to the bottom of it and rectify the matter because, in her opinion, wealthy heiresses shouldn't go traipsing around the countryside delving into things that might put them in danger.

"Oh," Henrietta exclaimed. "Evangeline has been

involved in numerous cases. In fact, I believe she is on first name terms with several detectives."

"Is that so? And where does Tom figure in your adventures?" Toodles asked, one eyebrow raised.

Henrietta laughed. "They are as thick as thieves. Evangeline does not go anywhere without him. Although… Now that I recall, there was that one instance when she trekked out to London by herself."

Toodles' fingers curled around the armrest. "And why, may I ask, wasn't Tom with you?" Toodles directed the question straight at Evie.

Henrietta laughed and took great delight in saying, "Evangeline gave him the slip." Turning to Evie, she added, "I have been having the most entertaining time going through those magazines your grandmother brought for you. There are all sorts of stories from damsels in distress, which I can take or leave, to gangsters wielding revolvers and rascals trying to get away with murder and saying things like *being sent up the river* and *packing heat* and referring to women as *cake-eaters*, *broads* and *dolls*." Henrietta dabbed the edge of her eye with her lace handkerchief. "I puzzled over the term *cabbage* until I worked out they were referring to money."

To Evie's relief, Henrietta's response managed to distract her granny.

"Well, at least someone is reading them," Toodles said. "I had to sacrifice an entire trunk to accommodate those magazines you wanted. Don't they have them here in England?"

"I'm sorry to have deprived you of an extra trunk, Granny. I can assure you, I will get around to reading them." In reality, Evie wanted to look at the pictures and advertisements. It seemed every day, someone came up with a new time saving gadget…

"I'm rather enjoying the advertisements," Henrietta said, almost as if she'd read Evie's mind. Pressing the tip of her finger against her chin, she looked up, "Let me think. Oh, yes… *Housekeepers can rest if they take advantage of labor-savers such as Campbell's Beans*. They advise buying them by the case." She turned to Toodles. "Do you eat beans with tomato sauce, Virginia?"

"Oh, please call me Toodles."

Henrietta blinked.

Evie could well imagine Henrietta asking, *must I?*

"As for your question, yes. I love beans on toast. In fact, we had some on our recent camping trip."

"Camping trip?"

Henrietta's puzzlement made Evie smile.

Toodles brightened. "It's a lot of fun. You should try it sometime. There's nothing like the fresh air you breathe in the wilderness. An entire troop of us descended upon the Elliot's camping ground last spring. They had these quaint log cabins built for the occasion on some land they'd purchased down south. Every night we sat by the campfire and sang songs and told stories." Toodles smiled. "Oh, I can still hear the crackling of those logs. And those stars in the sky…" She sighed. "They were magnificent."

Henrietta now looked confused. "These log cabins you speak of, did they have all the amenities?"

"They were quite rustic but they had everything we needed." Toodles spread her arms out. "And, of course, we had the woods, my dear."

"I see." Henrietta continued to look mystified and she

dealt with it by turning to Evie. "Did I tell you about the advertisement I saw for shoes?

Jumping at the opportunity to maintain the topic of conversation away from murder, Evie shook her head. "Were they nice shoes?"

"Oh, I suppose so, yes. Apparently, you can purchase them straight from a catalogue." Henrietta laughed. "Imagine that."

"Where do you get your shoes from, Henrietta?" Toodles asked.

Evie recognized the reservation in her granny's tone. It suggested Toodles harbored a few opinions, which she wished to express because she most likely assumed Henrietta would hold an opinion contrary to her own.

Henrietta gave her a most imperious look softened by her smile. "They are made by a craftsman in London. In fact, I have placed an order for some more shoes for next year."

"Next year? That's thinking ahead."

"That's when they will be ready," Henrietta explained.

Sensing the conversation might take a turn for the worse, Evie jumped to her feet and asked, "Would anyone like to join me in a game of croquet?"

They all looked at her, their smiles full of indulgence.

"At the rate you go through your opponents, we don't dare," Henrietta said. "Oh, I just remembered. Every other page in that magazine had advertisements for motor cars, or tires… It made me want to rush out and purchase a new motor car."

"But not the shoes?" Toodles asked, her tone declaring she had taken exception to Henrietta's remark.

Her granny lived in the lap of luxury but she could not

tolerate anyone looking down their noses at what she considered to be the salt of the earth people who labored long and hard for less than the bare essentials through no fault of their own. Although, at times, she argued everyone had the opportunity to better their situation regardless of who they were or where they came from...

"Oh, look," Evie exclaimed, "the others are returning from their stroll around the park." Evie hoped Henrietta and Toodles took that as a suggestion to behave themselves. She nodded to the footman standing nearby. "Would anyone like some more tea? Yes, I think we'll have some tea."

"Evangeline, anyone would think you are still fretting over Mr. Hartigan. You seem to be quite on edge."

"It's this business of hosting people," Evie admitted. "I want them to enjoy themselves and take away fond memories of their stay here but that is not always guaranteed."

As the footman walked off to organize the tea, Evie saw Edgar emerging from the house. Her butler walked with determination and then, to her surprise, he nearly tripped over his own feet.

Evie instantly knew the reason why.

He had spotted Miss Clara Ashwood. The stage actress had arrived a week before taking the entire household by surprise because Evie had forgotten to alert anyone of her arrival.

At first, Edgar had been speechless. Once he had fully recovered from the shock of seeing his favorite actress in person, he had jumped into action commanding the footmen as if they were his own private army, which in a sense they were.

While he had eventually managed to compose himself, he had been suffering momentary lapses. Evie put it down to his deep admiration of the thespian.

"My lady," he said as he reached her. "The doctor has just arrived and is asking for Miss Clara Ashwood."

Glancing over at her guests, Evie saw the actress break away from the group and head toward the house. Evie had only recently met the thespian who had come to Halton House to recuperate from a debilitating bout of something or other, which had taken hold of her whilst rehearsing for the lead role in Phillipa's debut play, which they would all be attending in a few days' time.

Edgar clasped his hands together and stood there staring at Clara Ashwood.

"Edgar. Are you breathing?"

"My apologies, my lady..." he broke off, his tone distracted because he had clearly fallen under Miss Clara Ashwood's spell.

"Was there anything else, Edgar?"

Edgar remained absorbed by the sight of the woman who commanded audiences and held them captivated by nothing more than her presence. "Roses," he finally said, his tone sounding distracted.

"Yes? What about them?"

"George Mills has informed me we are fresh out of red roses."

"How can that be? I'm sure I saw a profusion of them only a few days ago. In fact, red roses are George Mills' pride and joy." Her gardener took particular care of them as they always won him awards at the local flower shows.

"My lady, I would not have bothered you with such a

trite matter, but…" Edgar drifted off again, his eyes pinned on Clara Ashwood.

"Edgar!"

Startled, her butler cleared his throat and apologized.

"You mentioned roses," Evie prompted him.

"I did?"

"Yes."

He again apologized, saying, "I did not mean to bother you with the problem."

"Well, now that you have mentioned it, could you please explain it?"

"Very well, my lady. Soon after Miss Clara's arrival, Miss Phillipa telephoned to say Miss Clara enjoyed red roses in her room so I took it upon myself to ensure a vase with a dozen red roses was placed in her room every day."

Evie pictured the extensive rose gardens. Beyond that, George Mills had devoted more than an acre to his roses and other flowers for the specific use of the house and the parish church. Perhaps the demand had exceeded his supply…

"I see and now we are all out of red roses."

He nodded. "I shall, of course, do my utmost to find an alternative supplier."

Even if it meant scouring the countryside for the blooms, Evie guessed. "Well, do what you must, Edgar. We wouldn't want to disappoint Clara Ashwood."

He spoke as if in a trance. "No, indeed. We wouldn't." He bowed and hurried after the actress.

When Evie rejoined the others, Sara asked, "What in heavens is wrong with your butler? Is he drunk?"

Glancing his way, Evie saw him again tripping over his

own two feet. "He's a theater buff and appears to be somewhat awestruck." Evie couldn't help wondering if she had reason to be concerned.

"I thought English butlers were supposed to be stuffy and above such things," Toodles remarked.

"My butler happens to be eccentric." And, in a relationship of sorts with Millicent, her lady's maid, Evie thought. Not long ago, Edgar and Millicent had become an item. She would hate for anything to come between them. Even a fleeting infatuation could be fatal in a new relationship...

"Your guests must be quite taken with the park," Henrietta observed, "I believe they are about to trek off again."

Evie breathed a sigh of relief. Despite the dowagers stepping in to help her entertain the intimate group of people she had invited to stay at Halton House, since the arrival of the first guest she had been yearning to enjoy a moment alone. It didn't make sense...

The house party had been her idea. Since the age of eighteen, she had attended at least one house party a month. She had been looking forward to hosting a gathering for quite some time. At least, she had been saying so.

Henrietta's laughter snapped Evie out of her senseless reverie. Smiling, she asked, "What did I miss?"

It took a moment for Henrietta to compose herself. "We shouldn't laugh at Evangeline's expense, but wouldn't it be funny?"

"Oh, do share," Evie encouraged.

Recovering, Henrietta patted Evie's hand. "The recounting of the tale wouldn't seem so amusing now."

"You can't leave me in the dark," Evie complained.

Exchanging a look with Toodles and Sara, Henrietta sighed and said, "Speaking of advertisements, I recalled seeing one for a lady detective in one of our local papers. Imagine that, I thought at the time. Yet now…" Henrietta laughed again. "I can well imagine you advertising your services. Evangeline Parker, Lady Detective. Are you worried? If so, consult me. Private enquiries and delicate matters undertaken anywhere with secrecy and ability. Let me see, what else did they mention? Oh, yes. Divorce and *shadowings*. I take it that means following people. You could consult with your thespian friends. They might give you some ideas about disguising yourself."

A lady detective.

A quick glance at her granny told her she wasn't as amused by the idea as Henrietta seemed to be.

"Oh, look," Henrietta chortled. "I believe Evangeline is thinking about it."

Evie glanced at her grandmother but couldn't tell if she approved or disapproved of the proposal.

"This lady detective has offices in Curzon Street." Turning to Toodles, Henrietta explained, "That is in Mayfair. What you would refer to as the ritzy part of town. So you see, it would not be so demeaning if Evangeline set herself up in a detecting business."

Instead of objecting, Evie decided to go with the flow. "Only so long as I keep my title out of it."

"Of course, my dear. I am sure you would manage it well enough. You could keep it secret. It's become quite fashionable for ladies to undertake a profession without anyone knowing about it." Henrietta looked into the distance. "I wonder if your guests are taking another turn of the park because they heard about your third attempt on Mr. Hartigan's life. Perhaps they fear one of them is about to meet their end."

"Henrietta. How could you?"

Henrietta laughed. "You mustn't look so surprised, Evangeline. It's bound to happen. Either here or nearby. Now or sometime in the near future."

"Are you seriously entertaining those ideas?"

"I must say, I would be inclined to feel slightly disappointed if something doesn't happen soon. Something other than another attempt on poor Mr. Wilfred Hartigan. After all, since your return to Halton House there have been quite a number of incidents but not a single one here at the house. While your involvement has been coincidental, one begins to wonder if you haven't developed a penchant for the thrill of the chase. You never did take to fox-hunting. Perhaps you have found something of greater interest and your focus on it acts as a beacon, attracting trouble." Henrietta turned to Toodles. "Evangeline has a knack for entertaining the most outlandish theories which have, on occasion, proven to be quite helpful in capturing the guilty parties."

Straightening, Evie stated, "No one is going to be killed, Henrietta. So, you can put that out of your mind."

The dowager gave her a whimsical smile. "You say that with so much confidence. Let's hope the Fates were distracted. You wouldn't want to tempt them…"

CHAPTER 2

*E*vie adjusted her earrings and looked up. "Caro."

"Yes, milady."

"Have you noticed Edgar's odd behavior?"

"Not even a blind person could fail to notice it, milady. Just today I saw him swirl around on the spot as if he didn't quite know in which direction to head. If you ask me, he is suffering from a severe case of infatuation."

Evie swung on her chair. "Please tell me that isn't so."

Caro gave a small shrug. "Millicent is quite amused by it all."

"She is?"

"Oh, yes."

"Do you mean to say she is not concerned?"

"Of course not. She knows it won't come to anything. Edgar is merely in awe of Miss Clara Ashwood. He can't believe she is flesh and blood, although what he imagined her to be I have no idea. Anyhow, the fact she is right here at Halton House has him gasping for breath. But that's not the worst of it. He has everyone on edge, making sure everything is perfect for Miss Ashwood. The Prince of Wales has dined here and I don't recall seeing Edgar so jittery and concerned something will go wrong."

"And you're sure Millicent is fine with it."

"Absolutely. She has Edgar wrapped around her little finger. Not that anyone would know it since they have both remained quite professional. I must say, Millicent has impressed me. It's almost as if she has grown up. I haven't once caught her looking at another man. The footmen are feeling deprived without her attention. Now, let's see what we can do with your hair. You've spent the better part of the day outdoors and it has gone all frizzy."

"Caro! If I didn't know better, I'd say you are scolding me."

Caro rested her hands on Evie's shoulders. "Did you remember to wear a hat?"

"Of course... Although, it kept getting in the way of my shots. So... there might have been a few times when I removed it." She had actually flung it away in frustration because Tom had whizzed through his game of croquet. She would bet anything *he* hadn't given any thought to letting *her* win.

"I think I can see a freckle. No... wait. There are two."

"Nonsense." Evie leaned forward and inspected her face in the mirror. "You are teasing me."

Caro shook her head and clicked her tongue in disapproval. "Don't be surprised if you wake up tomorrow morning and find your face covered with freckles. It would serve you right."

"How is all this helping my hair?"

Once Caro finished taming her mop of auburn hair, she settled a headband on Evie's head and spent some time adjusting it. "I don't think you need a necklace." She stood back and inspected the headband and black dress with tiny black beads forming a diamond pattern.

Looking at the mirror, Evie cast a longing look at the dress she had chosen in a cheerful shade of pink. "I still don't see why I can't wear that one."

"I've already told you, milady. Lady Stafford is wearing pink tonight."

"I'm not sure Helen would appreciate you spying on her."

"Milady, you know it's all for the greater good. How would you feel if you made your grand entrance and found yourself wearing the same dress as one of your guests?"

"It might be the same color as Lady Stafford's dress but I'm sure it's a different style. Since her husband had to sell their country pile, Helen Stafford has been living on a shoestring budget. She says Lord Stafford has their money all tied up in investments. Anyhow, while I'm sure we have already seen her full range of new dresses for the season, what if she's changed her mind at the last minute and decided to wear something else?"

"She won't."

"How can you be sure?"

"Because she sent her maid to spy on your dress selection. I think we would all save ourselves a lot of trouble if the ladies' maids got together and shared the information but that would spoil the fun."

Evie lowered her headband a notch only to have Caro raise it again. Reluctant to challenge her maid to a battle of wills, she let it go. "Did Miss Clara Ashwood say if she would be joining us tonight?" Since arriving, the actress had been dining alone in her room.

"Yes, the doctor was pleased with her improvement. The fresh country air has done her a world of good. Miss Phillipa will be pleased. Apparently, the understudy is not up to the task and Miss Phillipa feels the performance will suffer for it."

"When did you speak with her?"

"Miss Phillipa telephoned this afternoon but she didn't want to bother you."

"Oh, dear. I hope for Phillipa's sake Miss Ashwood recovers in time to perform on opening night. I'm sure Phillipa is relying on me to ensure she is well taken care of and fully recovered in time."

"You have provided Miss Ashwood with the ideal place in which to recover. I can't think what more you can do." Caro handed her a pair of black gloves.

Evie winced slightly. "I feel overdressed. It probably has to do with the fact I don't usually wear black. We need to rethink our choice for the dress I will wear on opening night."

"We?" Caro giggled.

Evie tipped her chin up. "Granted, your tastes in clothes are superior and I know you have your heart set on me wearing a black gown, but I'm going to put my foot down."

Caro shook her head. "Black shows off your jewels. As you said, it's opening night. You'll be wearing your tiara and the Woodridge diamond necklace."

Both of which would need to be retrieved from the London bank where they were stored, Evie thought. It seemed such a nuisance… Evie's eyes narrowed slightly. "I want something cheerful. Green and… orange."

Caro's eyebrows shot up. "You might be hard pressed to find a dressmaker who will readily use that color combination."

"Well, I want it and… that's that. Please have a word with Mrs. Green. I'm sure she will oblige me."

"In a week?"

Evie worried the edge of her lip. She could picture green and orange and, in her opinion, it would look fabulous. A moment later, she regained her confidence and straightened. "Yes. Mrs. Green can work miracles. I trust her."

Shrugging, Caro said, "I'll let her know tomorrow morning and then watch her break into hives." Caro handed her a bottle of perfume. She watched her for a long moment and then asked, "Is something the matter, milady?"

"Apart from you being quite contrary? No."

"Are you sure? You seem to be in a combative mood. It's unlike you to push to have your way."

"Well, perhaps it's time I do have my way." Evie held a straight face for as long as she could before she broke into a worried smile. "Heavens. I think there is something wrong with me." Earlier, she had spent a considerable amount of time arguing with herself over the merits of winning or losing a game of croquet. Now, she had tried to interfere with Caro's dress selection when, in reality, she was relieved she never had to bother about such matters.

"Are your guests giving you trouble or is it your grandmother?"

"No. Everyone is being perfectly lovely."

"Can the same be said about you, milady?"

"Caro! What have you heard?"

Grinning, Caro admitted to witnessing Evie's attack on poor Mr. Hartigan. "Anyone would think you have developed a severe dislike to him."

Had she? "Now that you mention it, there is something dreadfully obvious about him. He struts about like a peacock showing off his fine feathers. Ordinarily, that wouldn't bother me, but the dowagers are making quite a big deal about him."

"They only want to see you happy."

"That's what I thought at first. Now I'm not so sure. This afternoon Henrietta suggested I had gathered the guests in order to bump one of them off. I'm sure she only means to amuse herself at my expense."

"Maybe that's the reason why you are on edge," Caro suggested.

"Oh, not you too. I am not on edge," Evie huffed. "Well, perhaps a little. And, if truth be known, I'm concerned about the possibility of something going wrong. Can you imagine what everyone will say? I didn't know it when I organized the invitations, but I hear the newspaper owner, Mr. Martin Gate, is in need of a newsworthy event. His sales for the quarter are down. I fear he might use me to prop up his newspaper. I should hate to become the target of his next front page." Evie jumped to her feet. "I will just have to make sure everyone has the dullest time possible."

Smiling, Caro said, "That's the spirit, milady. Only… do remember to keep your distance from Mr. Hartigan."

As the mantle clock struck the hour, someone

knocked on her door. Caro opened it to reveal Evie's granny fidgeting with her necklace.

"Ah, Birdie. You're still here. Then again, according to your itinerary, there is still half an hour before drinks are served." She produced a small flask. "But I have come prepared." She strode in and settled herself at the foot of the bed. Looking up at Caro, she smiled. "Could I have a moment alone with my granddaughter, please?"

Caro made a wordless exit leaving Evie to fret over what her grandmother might want to talk about. Since her arrival several days before, Evie had been avoiding being left alone with her. She should have known Toodles would find a way around that.

"You're looking… very grown up in that gown. I don't think I have ever seen you wearing black, not even when you were in mourning."

"Nicholas didn't care for it and he made me promise I wouldn't succumb to pressure."

"So why are you wearing it now?"

Evie rolled her eyes. "Caro likes it. She thinks it makes me look like a Countess. All right and proper and whatnot."

Toodles looked around the room. "Nothing ever changes here."

"Why should it?"

"Because the rest of the world is changing. You even have the same furniture."

"You know I'm only a custodian. Oh, wait a minute, we now have a wireless and the telephone. In fact, we have two telephones installed at Halton House. They weren't here when you last visited." Knowing her granny appreciated cutting to the chase, Evie threw caution to the wind and asked, "Is there something specific you wanted to talk to me about?"

"This business of you and Tom..." Toodles studied the flask and then put it away in her small silk bag.

Evie's mind flooded with a million questions and, quite suddenly, emptied.

Toodles continued, "I take it he is no longer your chauffeur."

"Oh… No, he's not." Evie shrugged. "Granny, it's a long story."

"And what exactly does that mean? Are you two an item?" Evie must have looked confused enough for Toodles to say, "I know I disapproved of your marriage to the Earl but I thought he was after your money. Don't roll your eyes at me, missy. Plenty of girls walked down the aisle for the simple purpose of bankrolling some lord's manor house restoration."

"Granny, if you recall, many of those girls were refused entry into society back home because their money was too new. I applaud them for looking else-where. I guess it's now your turn to roll your eyes at me."

"Did you know your great-aunt Cecily has named you sole beneficiary in her will? You've already cashed in a couple of inheritances and you're a beneficiary of three more, four if you count mine but I'm still tossing around the idea of erecting a vast monument to myself." Toodles gave a firm nod. "Anyhow, I witnessed it and you know Cecily never changes her mind. That will make you wealthier than the rest of us combined. The old biddy hasn't spent a dime in years. And that brings me to another matter. The only reason she's leaving you her money is because she never married and had children."

"And your point is?"

"I hired Tom to make sure no one took advantage of you."

That was the point she'd been trying to make? What did Tom have to do with Evie not marrying again? "Rest assured, he is doing his job."

"Is that all he's doing?" Toodles asked.

"Did Henrietta fill you in on my murder investigations?" Suddenly, the subject she had been avoiding seemed more palatable than talking about what might be going on or not between her and Tom. Evie couldn't explain the surge of defensiveness she felt. Suffice to say, if she happened to fall in love with Tom, no one would stand in her way. Least of all her granny who would no doubt threaten to cut her off.

After a long moment, Toodles smiled from ear to ear. "You mean to say she wasn't pulling my leg?"

"Why are you smiling?" Earlier, when Henrietta had jested about Evie becoming a lady detective, Toodles had given her the impression she disapproved.

"I'm just picturing your mother's reaction. She is always complaining you took after me."

"Is that good or bad?" Evie asked cautiously.

Toodles patted her cheek. "You have the courage to defy your boundaries. I'd say that is good. I could not be prouder of you. Now, tell me about one of your adventures."

Not quite believing her granny's unexpected acceptance, Evie gave her a brief account of the last case she had been involved in.

"The Countess of Woodridge, a detective." Toodles laughed.

"It's not like that, Granny. I just happen to be in the right place… or the wrong place at the right time. I didn't go looking for trouble." Frowning, Evie said, "You're supposed to give me a lecture now about putting myself in danger."

Toodles looked around the room and gave a pensive shake of her head. "The thought of you withering away in this mausoleum has given me more sleepless nights than I care to count. Tom will look after you, I'm sure."

"You're not cross with me?"

"It warms my heart to know you are putting your skills, whatever they might be, to good use. Every day I hear about someone's daughter or granddaughter doing something remarkable." Toodles gave her a brisk smile. "This gives me hope."

Before her granny could ruin the moment by saying she would much rather see Evie married with a brood of children, Evie asked, "What about Tom? Are you going to give him a piece of your mind?"

"Oh, absolutely. I need to keep him on his toes. He has to earn his keep."

Something about the way Toodles looked askance set warning bells off. Her granny's mind worked in mysterious ways. Evie thought about prodding but then Toodles changed the subject.

"Now I remember what I came in here to ask. Are you on some sort of slimming diet?"

"No."

"Well, then… where's the sugar? Every dessert I've had here has been sorely lacking in sweetness."

"Oh…" Evie gave her an apologetic smile. "We're still on rations."

"Rations? But it's been nearly two years since the end of the war. You might have mentioned something. Instead of carting all those magazines over for you, I could have loaded up the trunk with sugar."

"Sorry. We've become so accustomed to it, it didn't even occur to ask. Anyway, things are slowly but surely starting to get back to normal. I'm sure we'll soon have more sugar than we'll know what to do with."

Evie inspected her reflection and adjusted her hairband, lowering it a little the way she thought it should sit. After a second, she nudged it back into place. "Perhaps we should make our way down." She turned just as someone knocked on the door.

Edgar entered. "My apologies for interrupting, my lady."

"What is it Edgar?"

"It's the roses, my lady. There has been a development."

Toodles clapped her hands. "Is this a mystery?"

"As a matter of fact, madam, yes."

Toodles turned to Evie. "Madam? Do I look like a madam to you?"

Edgar's cheeks colored. He looked at Evie for guidance.

"It's fine, Edgar. You should play it safe and just address my granny as Toodles. I know it might cause you some discomfort, but trust me, you don't want to hear about Americans being addressed as madam."

"Very well, my lady."

"The development, Edgar."

"Oh, yes. One of the stable boys reported seeing someone from the house stepping out in the middle of the night. Without a moon to see by, he couldn't tell if it was a man or a woman, but he said they went straight for the rose garden. At the time, he thought it might have been one of your guests going out for an assignation." Edgar cleared his throat. "George Mills didn't want to say anything but the fact of the matter is… Someone hacked the roses off."

"Hacked?" Evie glanced at her granny and saw her look of surprise turn to concern. Evie could well imagine her wondering where Tom had been while her roses had been hacked.

"Birdie, don't you have someone doing the rounds of the estate? Someone like a night watchman?"

"Granny, this isn't Belvoir Castle. We have someone at the gatehouse. He keeps an eye on things but he can hardly be expected to be everywhere at once."

"You've lost me. What does Belvoir Castle to do with Halton House?"

"It's a grander estate."

"Yes, but I would bet anything you are the one with the greatest fortune."

"The one only you and I and a handful of family members know about?"

They both turned and looked at Edgar who in turn looked up at the ceiling.

Toodles shook her head. "And still, you're the one with people wandering around hacking your roses. Makes one wonder what else they might get up to." Toodles retrieved her flask, raised it in a toast, and took a swift drink. "Looks like you have a mystery on your hands. What are you going to do now? Round up all the suspects?"

"Granny! I can't go around suspecting my guests?"

"Why not? One of them obviously doesn't like your roses."

Evie turned to Edgar. "Thank you. I'll… I'll have a word with George Mills tomorrow morning."

"That's it?" Toodles stared at her, eyes wide, mouth gaping open. "What if the culprit used the roses as a practice run? What if we're next? Exactly how well do you know your guests?"

CHAPTER 3

Wilfred Hartigan – Publisher
Horace Gibbins – Theater critic
Lady Manners (Loulou) –Evie's long-time friend
Lady Stafford (Helen) – A peer without a country house
Clara Ashwood – Thespian, recuperating at Halton House
Lauren Wilkes – Silent movie star
Martin Gate – Newspaper owner

The drawing room, Halton House

Despite making Toodles promise she wouldn't bring up the subject of the hacked roses, Evie knew she would need to keep a close eye on her granny or risk her turning the incident into the main topic of conversation during dinner.

Evie smiled across the room and made eye contact with Wilfred Hartigan. No hard feelings, she thought, happy to see the publisher conversing with the Hollywood star, Lauren Wilkes. She had already overheard him suggesting the actress should keep a journal as it would eventually keep her because everyone loved a tell all book.

Did anyone know about Clara Ashwood's love of roses? Evie glanced at the Hollywood star. Would Lauren Wilkes have reason to deprive the stage actress of roses? They were both in the same profession. That made them perfect candidates for jealousy or some sort of rivalry.

Toodles had asked how well she knew her guests...

Not well at all, Evie thought.

What if Clara Ashwood and Lauren Wilkes had a history of animosity or rivalry?

Continuing to make the rounds of the drawing room, Evie saw Horace Gibbins, the theater critic, stake his place beside Toodles. It took him a moment to accommodate his large frame on the dainty sofa. When he finally made himself comfortable, he gave Toodles a bright smile filled with self-confidence and a hint of conceit, using his unique nasal tone to say, "Mrs. Otway-Wells, I hear you have been traveling."

Toodles looked up from her glass of whisky. "I beg your pardon, were you talking to me?"

"I believe so, yes."

"Then you must call me Toodles."

"Toodles. Magnificent. How did you ever come by that moniker?"

"...Let me think, it first started with me saying toodle-oo whenever someone irked me. I didn't know it at the time, but I had adopted it as my standard way of getting rid of dull company. However, other people noticed and, over time, the name stuck and became Toodles."

"Why, I believe we are about to become the best of friends," Horace Gibbins declared.

"I guess I must have told the story wrong," Toodles murmured.

Evie rolled her eyes and turned to Edgar. "Edgar, I believe I shall have a Gibson, hold the Vermouth, please."

"Certainly, my lady. One pickled onion or two?"

"Hold the onions too, please."

The edge of his lip quivered before he drawled out in a tone hinting at disapproval, "One glass of gin, coming right up."

She turned in time to see her granny deliver an impish smile.

"Say, aren't you the fellow who makes a habit of making women cry?" Toodles didn't wait for Horace Gibbins to respond. "Yes, you are. I read your last review. I'm surprised you don't get around with a bodyguard. Do you sleep with a revolver under your pillow?"

Not sounding the least bit offended by her granny's remark, the theater critic said, "As much as I am despised by some and feared by others, I am equally revered by those who appreciate an honest appraisal."

"If memory serves," Toodles said, "you recently told a starlet she would be wise to land herself a husband before the season is over, and I'm sure you did not mean to refer to the London season but rather, the play season."

Horace Gibbins leaned in and murmured *sotto voce*, "I believe she has already secured a husband as that had been her intention all along."

"That seems to please you. I can't help thinking you

have deprived her of a career. Do you think I hatched into this magnificent specimen of womanhood overnight? No, *siree*. It takes time to hone one's skills. Now, we will never know how good she might have been."

Horace Gibbins chortled. "I must say, it's refreshing to hear a woman championing another woman's cause."

"You have obviously been speaking with the wrong people. Anyone who heard you would think women are their own worst enemies."

"In my experience," he parried, "yes, they are. Especially when they are vying for the same position. I have yet to meet a single understudy who wouldn't consider killing the star of the show just to have a chance to play the leading role. I believe that applies to every woman."

Toodles downed the contents of her drink and prepared to give Horace Gibbins a piece of her mind.

Evie searched for Tom and found him leaning against a bookcase, his eyes sparkling with amusement. She drew his attention and nudged her head toward her granny. Tom responded with a shrug of his shoulders. Evie's eyebrows slammed together. That prompted Tom to straighten. With a small nod and what looked like a sigh of resignation, he wove his way across the drawing room and did his best to interject before Toodles hit a high note in her speech.

Disaster averted, Evie thought.

Tom cleared his throat. "Toodles, I believe you were about to regale us with one of your travel tales."

"Yes, indeed. I was just about to tell this fine gentleman all about my voyage over here."

Evie lowered herself into a chair. She knew Toodles had found a different weapon of choice and was about to deliver some just desserts, commanding Mr. Gibbins' attention until she wore him out or bored him to death.

"It all began one fine spring morning several months back. We motored all the way from Newport, Rhode Island to Plymouth where my son keeps one of his yachts. From there, we sailed down to Manhattan. I keep telling him he should get a bigger boat so we can sail straight here, but he won't hear of it. Something about speed or whatnot…"

The last time Evie had seen her granny ensnare an unwitting victim who knew better than to walk away, it had taken Toodles an entire hour to sail away from New York and work her way through all the passengers she had encountered along the way.

Seeing her green eyes glinting with satisfaction, Evie knew her granny was leaving nothing out. She gave Mr. Gibbins a brief glance, enough to see his eyes had already glazed over, suggesting her granny was going into great detail, describing everything from the lace on the ladies' gowns to their entire family trees. Since her granny had a knack for making stories up on the spot, she would plump up the family trees with characters of her own making.

Clearly, she did not like Mr. Gibbins.

A brief survey of the room assured Evie everyone else was engaged in conversation and had been offered refreshments.

Glancing away, Evie saw Henrietta sitting stock-still, her eyes not even blinking as she watched Toodles. Evie could only imagine the trepidation coursing through the dowager at the prospect of sitting through the entire diatribe.

Edging toward her, Evie asked, "Henrietta. Would you like me to refresh your drink?"

"I think you might need to, Evangeline. What is your grandmother thinking? Doesn't she know who that is?"

"Yes, I'm afraid she's fully aware and therein lies the challenge. I suspect she is taunting him into printing something about her in his column. I sent Tom over but I think he only managed to stoke the fire." And now, he too had to sit through the discourse. Evie could barely hide her smile.

"Whatever possessed you to invite the gentleman?" Henrietta asked. "I hear he wields his pen with wrathful vengeance."

"Oh, so you have read his opinion column."

"Yes. And I can see him composing his next piece as we speak."

"You know, he's also the theater critic and… Well, Toodles is putting on quite a performance. I invited him as a special favor to Phillipa. Although, I can't imagine his visit here will sway him to give Phillipa's play a favorable review."

"Wouldn't she prefer an honest appraisal?" Henrietta asked.

"Yes, but Mr. Gibbins is not known for his honesty. Unfortunately, he prefers to be courted."

"But that is dreadful. Someone should do something about it."

"Yes, indeed." Mr. Gibbins had arrived a couple of days before but had kept to himself saying the journey had fatigued him. Evie hadn't understood how he could have been tired since he had only traveled from London. But then Caro had told her Mr. Gibbins had enquired about

Miss Ashwood and upon being told the thespian was spending her time in her room, he had decided to withdraw to his own room emerging that morning but only after being told Miss Ashwood had decided to breakfast with the rest of the guests.

Strangely, Evie had as yet to see him engage Miss Ashwood in conversation. So far, he had spent the evening admiring her from afar. Earlier that day, when the guests had taken a walk around the park, Mr. Gibbins had walked two paces behind but his attention had clearly been on the actress.

Did Edgar have a rival?

"I must say, whatever feeling of apprehension I felt about your grandmother's visit seems to have been misplaced. She is still the same person, so I have to assume I have come to see her in a new light. Either that or time has withered away my prejudices. Perhaps I have become more tolerant without even realizing it. I will have to give it some more thought."

Evie gaped at her.

"Oh, don't look so surprised, Evangeline. I may appear to be set in my ways, but there is something to be said for a breath of fresh air and your grandmother is providing that." Henrietta scanned the room. "Lady Stafford is managing to keep up appearances but the loss of Stafford Hall has definitely taken its toll on her. I can't help but feel she has lost her joyful vivacity. Now I'm ridden with guilt because I have been trying to avoid her. What does one say to someone who has been forced out of their ancestral home?"

"It's not the end of the world, Henrietta. Besides, it was Lord Stafford's ancestral home, not Helen's, and they still have their London house." Evie studied her for a moment. "I don't think Helen looks downcast. The fact she accepted the invitation tells me she has come to terms with her new circumstances. Although, I hope Lord Stafford will eventually recover."

Henrietta gave a mournful sigh. "I doubt it. If you recall, they were here when news of his brother's death reached them. Lord Stafford's breath rushed out and his face whitened. Heavens, to have died only forty-eight hours before the Armistice. I saw Lord Stafford in town recently. Even after all this time, he still looks in shock. In any case, a peer without a country house is beyond my realm of comprehension."

Evie tried to picture Helen Stafford hacking away at the roses. Why would she? When she couldn't come up with a reason for the vicious act, she dismissed it. "They're not the only ones to survive without a country estate. Most of the peers choosing to sell their country homes have prestigious London homes in Mayfair or Park Lane or Regent's Park."

Henrietta mused, "Not everyone is choosing to sell. Some are being forced into it." She took a sip of her drink and nodded. "You might be right about Lady Stafford. She's bearing up quite well. But, in her place, I would probably go into hiding." Henrietta shivered. "There is far too much of this going on. I still remember seeing the notice for the Sutton Scarsdale estate last year. The magnificent Georgian house, the local pub, thirty farms and seventy houses, cottages and shops, all offered for sale. No one wanted the large house."

"Oh, I think I remember hearing something about it,"

Evie offered. "Didn't someone buy the house as a country retreat?"

Henrietta shook her head. "No. It didn't stand a chance. Apparently, it was simply too far from London. So sad. A syndicate of local businessmen purchased it and gutted the place. Can you imagine it? They stripped the lead from its roof and sold off its fittings to a London antiques dealer." She looked around the sumptuous drawing room. "That such a fate should befall upon us…"

"It won't," Evie assured her. "Nicholas took care of that."

Henrietta shifted in her seat and turned her attention to Lady Manners.

Evie did not, for a single moment, suspect Lady Manners of hacking her roses.

Evie had met the petite brunette during her first stay in London. Lady Manners's spirited manner had helped Evie navigate her way through a society that had seemed far too restrained for her liking. When Evie had returned home to America shortly after the war, Lady Manners had visited her. Widowed during the Great War, she had wanted to escape and had considered settling in a foreign land. In the months she had spent with Evie, she had received no less than three marriage proposals, all from wealthy gentlemen offering her a life of leisure, but Loulou, as Evie had come to know her, had wanted to pursue a different lifestyle. To this day, Evie had no idea if she had succeeded in finding something to engage her interest. Every time she asked her, Loulou would shrug and say she had become a work in progress.

"Martin Gate is showing a great deal of interest in

Lady Manners," Henrietta said. "I hope something comes of it. We haven't attended a wedding in ages."

Martin Gate needed an interesting story for his newspaper. Would he choose the malicious destruction of roses for his front page?

Evie studied the couple for a moment. "Yes, now that you mention it, I'm sure he swapped place cards last night. I could have sworn he'd been allocated a place next to Lauren Wilkes."

"Tell me again how you know the Hollywood star," Henrietta said.

"She's a new acquaintance. Phillipa introduced her to me a while back. Lauren has only recently returned from America where she made quite a career in Hollywood working in silent movies. Now she wishes to become a stage actress."

Henrietta hummed under her breath. "I wish someone would hurry up and invent talking movies. I simply don't understand why it hasn't been done yet. We have the wireless radio. Couldn't they simply use the same idea? I find reading dialogue rather awkward. Despite trying my best to inject the right tone, I still hear my own voice." Henrietta tilted her head and turned her attention back to Lady Manners. "Something about Lady Manners is slightly off but I can't put my finger on it. Have you noticed anything different about her?"

Evie took a sip of her drink and shifted her attention from the Hollywood movie star to Loulou. "She has been quieter than usual, but not withdrawn. In fact, every time I see her, she's sitting with someone new. But she doesn't appear to be saying very much."

"I hope for your sake she hasn't sunk into some sort of

depression," Henrietta murmured. "She has always been a great conversationalist."

"I've always known her to be witty, but I find she's more inclined to ask questions that lead one to do all the talking."

Henrietta chortled. "And that is what makes her such a wonderful conversationalist. There's nothing more awkward than when a person hogs a conversation."

Evie smiled. "Isn't that a contradiction? At least one person has to do the talking."

Henrietta clicked her fingers. "I believe she is studying people. Yes, that's what I've noticed about her. She's sitting right here with us, but she might as well be in the background."

"Oh, you might be right. What do you think that's about?"

Henrietta shivered again. "She might be plotting to kill someone."

"Henrietta! You are obsessed."

"Just look at her. She's listening to Mr. Martin Gate, but she has the look of someone whose mind is miles away. Now that I think about it. Earlier today, I saw her scribbling something on a notebook. When she heard me approaching, she slipped the notebook inside her handbag and pretended to be looking for something."

"How do you know she wasn't?"

Henrietta lifted her chin. "She looked guilty."

"I'm beginning to think you are bored and in desperate need of entertainment. That reminds me… You had a great deal of fun at my expense today. I had been trying to keep Toodles in the dark and you had to go and spill the beans."

Henrietta gave her a sheepish smile. "Virginia was bound to hear about it all sooner or later."

"Yes, well, and now she's giving Tom a thorough dressing down. How am I going to make amends?"

Glancing over at Toodles, Henrietta laughed. "Yes, she is definitely giving Tom a piece of her mind. And look, Mr. Horace Gibbins looks quite relieved. He's off the hook now. There he goes. He's making his escape. I hope he doesn't come this way. There's something odd about that man. He definitely needs more than a few days in the country. Look at his skin. It's all pasty and wearing that red rose on his buttonhole doesn't help. It makes him look even paler."

Frowning, Evie wondered how he had come by that red rose. She considered telling Henrietta about their red rose problem when Edgar announced dinner.

One by one, they stood up and began moving toward the dining room only to come to a stop when someone shrieked.

Turning, Evie saw the stage actress, Clara Ashwood, looking down at her silver dress. Or rather, staring open-mouthed at the stain on the front of her dress.

For a wild moment, Evie thought she had been shot. But then a footman rushed toward her, a cloth in hand.

Someone had spilled their drink on Clara.

Lady Stafford stepped up. "Oh, dear. I am so sorry."

And yet, she didn't sound the least bit remorseful.

CHAPTER 4

To her credit, Clara Ashwood insisted they carry on and not wait for her. As Clara hurried away to change her gown, Evie asked the dowager to take over while she followed the actress upstairs.

"I hope it doesn't leave a stain," Evie said. When they reached Clara Ashwood's room, she rang for one of the maids. Thankfully, Caro knocked on the door and entered.

"Do you have something else to change into?" Evie asked.

Clara Ashwood gave her a tight smile and nodded.

Caro took that as a signal to inspect the actress' wardrobe. After a brief search, she drew out a black dress.

So much for not wanting her to wear the same color as one of her guests, Evie thought.

"I'm sorry to have made such a fuss," the actress offered. "I'm sure it was an accident."

Evie noticed the same lack of conviction she had heard

in Lady Stafford's tone. Although, in Lady Stafford's case, it had been a lack of remorse…

If it hadn't been an accident, then it had been a deliberate attack. But what could have prompted that?

When Caro finished helping her dress, she bundled up the stained gown saying, "This should be ready for tomorrow, Miss Ashwood. You needn't concern yourself with it. It will be as good as new."

Clara smiled in appreciation. "If you don't mind, I'd like to spend a few moments alone."

"Of course." As Evie turned toward the door, she saw the vase of red roses. Edgar had clearly found another supplier.

Evie and Caro stepped out of the room. Waiting until they had reached the end of the hallway, Caro then asked, "What happened? She doesn't look at all happy."

"I didn't actually witness the incident, but I get the feeling Lady Stafford might have meant to spill her drink on Clara's dress."

"Why would she do that?"

"I don't know. I haven't heard anything that might give cause for concern. Otherwise, I would not have invited them to stay here at the same time." Evie put her hand on Caro's arm. "Do you think you could find out something? Perhaps the maids have heard a rumor."

"I'll do what I can."

"Well, that's a start. Lady Manners lives in London. She's always been a fount of knowledge. I'm sure if there is anything winding its way around the grapevine, she will have heard about it."

Evie entered the dining room to find everyone

enjoying their first course. One by one, her guests looked up and followed her progress to her chair beside Tom.

As Evie settled down, she said, "I don't remember placing you here. In fact, I'm certain I had organized to have Mr. Martin Gate sitting next to me tonight."

"Not while Toodles is here. From now on, I'm to stick to your side, no matter what."

"I see. You have been issued orders."

"It doesn't help that she's been reading about the troubles across the border. She seems to think you'll get in the way of a stray bullet." He looked up. "Which is actually my job. To get in the way, that is…"

Evie glanced across the table at Toodles. "Seriously? We could not be further away from the border." She frowned. "And why am I even questioning such a ludicrous suggestion?"

"I don't ask questions. Anyhow, what's the update on the dress? I take it there was nothing accidental about the drink being spilled on it?"

"I'm as much in the dark as you are. However, I've engaged Caro to do some digging around. There might be something going on between Clara Ashwood and Lady Stafford. Although I can't imagine what that something might be."

Tom stared at her for long minutes. "Do you suspect we might be in the midst of a scandal without even being aware of it?"

"I can't tell if you are laughing at my expense or worried on my behalf."

"Actually, I'm experiencing a strange sort of relief. The focus has been taken off you. For a while there, it looked as if you had lined up your guests to get rid of them, starting with Mr. Hartigan."

"Don't you start too."

"What do you mean?"

"Henrietta expressed a certain excitement over the possibility of me plotting against my guests. Not in so many words, but she has a way of hinting that leaves one in no doubt."

Edgar set her entrée down in front of Evie and hesitated slightly.

Glancing at him, Evie said, "Miss Clara Ashwood will be down momentarily, Edgar. So, you can relax. She has come to no harm."

"Thank you, my lady." Edgar stepped away only to hesitate.

"Edgar. She shouldn't be too long."

He nodded and resumed his place.

Evie looked up and across the table at Lady Stafford. Helen sat next to Martin Gate and they were carrying on a murmured conversation. If anyone could get information out of Helen, it would be the newspaper owner. Evie studied Helen's expression and decided she must be talking about her disdain for Clara Ashwood.

Drawing Tom's attention to them, she asked, "What do you think they are talking about?"

"Henrietta mentioned Lady Stafford's husband recently sold off their country estate," Tom said. "She could be bemoaning the fact she now has to rely on invitations."

Evie sighed. "This is so tiresome. Now I will have to contrive a way to get her to talk about the actress without sounding inquisitive. There's only one day to go before we head off to London so I should just ignore the incident but as the hostess it is my duty to ensure everyone is comfortable and happy."

"The newspaper owner is listening with rapt attention," Tom said. "She's definitely confiding in him. See how she leaned in? Oh, yes. That is the look of a woman imparting the sort of information she pretends she doesn't want spread around but is, in fact, hoping Mr. Gate will make sure everyone hears about the bad blood between the two women."

"Heavens, you are enjoying this."

"Now, we must figure out what transpired between the two women. Any suggestions?" he asked.

"I can't even begin to imagine what might have happened. It makes no sense. They went out walking together today."

"Maybe Miss Ashwood said something and Lady Stafford took offense but decided to restrain herself."

"And you think she then lost her control and spilled the drink on Clara Ashwood as some sort of belated retribution? Heavens, what if that was her way of throwing down the gauntlet?" Oh, she hoped not... It would be bad form to cause a scandal in someone else's home.

"We could be in for a bumpy night," Tom mused.

Having overheard Tom's remark, Lauren Wilkes said, "That sounds like a line that should be immortalized on the stage."

Evie sighed. "I need to contact Phillipa as soon as possible. If anything happens to Clara Ashwood, I will have a job and a half trying to clear the air."

"If there is something going on between the two ladies,

don't you think Phillipa would have warned you before-hand?" Tom asked.

"She didn't know I'd be inviting Lady Stafford. In any case, Phillipa has been short on information. In fact, she didn't even have much to say about Clara's illness. I still don't know what is wrong with her. Phillipa only said she needed a rest and some fresh country air to breath because she hadn't been feeling well."

The entrée plates were removed and Evie had to think long and hard to recall what she'd just eaten. She looked down at her empty wine glass. When had she drunk it?

She was about to say something when she noticed Tom was leaning away to speak to Lauren Wilkes. Evie remembered placing the Hollywood star next to Wilfred Hartigan. Had Tom captured the movie star's attention?

She waited for Edgar to set her main course down and said, "No one seems to be sitting where they are supposed to be, Edgar."

"No, my lady. When they entered the dining room, they were all deep in conversation. I'm afraid my efforts to guide them to their appropriate places fell on deaf ears."

"I'm sorry, Edgar. I know that must have caused you great distress." What could have possessed her guests? "At least everyone seems to have settled down." And, despite the earlier incident, they were all conversing with ease.

She turned to her left only to realize she hadn't even been aware of the person sitting there.

Horace Gibbins.

The theater critic sat back to allow a footman to refresh his glass of wine and then he resumed his conversation with Lady Manners who sat on his left.

Evie watched Loulou listening to the theater critic with what appeared to be complete fascination. Hoping they would have another theory about Lady Stafford and Clara Ashwood, Evie tried to eavesdrop on the conversation but she couldn't pick up on any of the words.

Leaning in slightly, Evie strained to hear something but the conversation mingled with everyone's chatter. At one point, Horace Gibbins smiled at her before lowering his voice even further and resuming his chat with Loulou.

Evie's attention drifted to Henrietta who sat to Loulou's left. The dowager was engaged in a lively conversation with Wilfred Hartigan. "I'm glad to see Wilfred has recovered," Evie said and assumed she had been talking to herself.

To her surprise, Tom laughed and said, "It took a good helping of your finest whisky to get Wilfred to finally breathe easy. I'm surprised he can hold himself upright. He has a whopping bruise on his knee."

Evie felt a rush of heat settle on her cheeks. "I hope he won't hold it against me."

"I doubt he holds a single memory of the event. He spent most of the afternoon sleeping it off. I had to get a footman to help him up to his room. Now that I think about it, I'm surprised he managed to get himself downstairs for dinner."

Evie whispered, "Did Lauren Wilkes have anything to say about the incident with the wine glass?"

Tom gave a small nod. "Yes, she just shared some intriguing information. There is talk of infidelity."

Evie gasped.

Lord Stafford? Henry... Unfaithful to Helen?

Impossible.

A wave of murmurs rose and then died down. Evie looked up and saw Clara Ashwood standing at the dining room door.

Her soft eyes swept around the room. Evie had heard her look described as love-in-the-mist eyes. With an almost ethereal presence, she moved with elegant grace toward her chair, a secretive smile in place.

She had changed her dress. Instead of wearing the black gown Caro had selected for her, she wore a plain elegant tunic dress with thin straps and a loose flowing diaphanous layer that resembled a peignoir.

"The lady in red," Tom mused. "I guess that confirms the rumors."

It took a moment for Evie to grasp the full meaning of what he'd said.

Too late, Evie realized Clara Ashwood had made her way to the only vacant chair available. Right next to Lady Stafford.

The two women shared a smile that might have fooled some people into believing they were the best of friends.

Without breaking eye contact, Helen held her empty glass of wine up. As a footman hurried to fill it up, Evie saw Edgar flapping his arms. Clearly, he recognized the danger in providing Lady Stafford with more ammunition.

It seemed everyone held their collective breaths and only exhaled when Lady Stafford took an appreciate sip and set her glass down.

Turning to Clara Ashwood, Lady Stafford complimented her dress before resuming her conversation with Martin Gate.

To Evie's relief, whatever had transpired between the

two women had been set aside either for the sake of propriety or because the matter had reached an impasse neither party wanted to or felt in any way compelled to challenge.

Evie wanted to believe peace had been restored. Even if it had, she suspected it would only be a temporary truce.

As much as she hoped the incident would all be forgotten, she knew it would eventually come up in conversation. But what if something even worse happened?

Horace Gibbins had always given Clara Ashwood glowing reviews for her performances. Would he be tempted to write a piece in his opinion column about the incident he'd witnessed at Halton House?

What if Martin Gate decided to use the incident to his advantage? She knew he wanted to increase circulation. That didn't necessarily mean he would focus on a news-worthy event. On the contrary. People liked to be enter-tained by gossip.

"Countess? Are you all right?" Tom asked.

"I'm suddenly tempted to announce our engagement." When he didn't answer, Evie turned to look at Tom. "Are you breathing?"

Tom reached for his glass of wine. "Did I miss something?"

"Diversionary tactics," she offered. "Such an announcement would take everyone's mind off my feuding guests."

"And focus their attention on us?"

Evie looked at Tom in time to see him take a deep

swallow. She burst out laughing. "Are you about to get on a boat back to America?"

"Did I hear you say you wanted to make an announcement?" Toodles asked.

"How does she do that?" Evie whispered. Blurting out the first idea that came to mind, Evie said, "I'll be hosting an opening night party at the theater. You are all invited."

"How gracious of you," Tom whispered. "If they don't kill each other here, they'll have another opportunity in London."

CHAPTER 5

"*I*'m sorry to drag you in here so early, Caro."
Evie sat up in bed and plumped up her pillows.
"I hardly slept a wink last night worrying about what
might happen during the night. Dare I ask?"

Caro nodded. "I performed a body count this morning,
milady. All is well. Everyone survived the night."

"I wish you wouldn't be so macabre, but are you sure?"

"Absolutely, milady. Despite the fine weather, since her
arrival, Miss Clara Ashwood has requested a fire in her
room to be lit before she wakes up. The maid went in
quite early and she reported seeing Miss Clara Ashwood
stirring awake. She then requested a cup of tea. I took it in
personally. She was alive and well."

"Your thoroughness is to be commended. Thank you,
Caro."

"Edgar spent the night on a chair at the end of the hall-
way," Caro continued. "I must say, this is probably the
very first house party where none of the guests left their
rooms during the night. I believe you have succeeded in

ensuring your guests had a thoroughly dull time of it. I wouldn't be surprised to find some of them barricaded themselves in during the night."

Evie poured herself a cup of tea. "That would be somewhat extreme. The only person who might have reason to be concerned is Clara Ashwood. Why would anyone else feel they were in danger?"

Caro smiled but refrained from commenting.

"Oh, I see. You think Wilfred Hartigan is afraid I might make another attempt on his life."

Again, Caro remained silent.

"Well, let me tell you, if anything else happens to him, I can hardly be held responsible. I didn't tell him to step into the path of the roadster and I certainly didn't tell him to stand in the direct line of my croquet ball. As for the hot tea... I have no idea what he was doing sitting so close to me. Anyhow, did you manage to get any information from the maids?"

"Nothing of real interest. Lady Manners's maid requested writing paper several times. Lady Manners might be writing a memoir or perhaps she feels she might be called upon to give evidence and needs to keep track of events."

Rather than comment on the absurdity of Caro's remark, Evie chose to focus on taking a nibble of her toast.

"What else have you discovered?" Evie asked.

"The Hollywood star, Lauren Wilkes, needs to get her act together. She leaves her clothes scattered about the place and seems to do it on purpose."

"How so?"

"Apparently, she'll hold something out and just let it

drop where it may."

"That's rude."

Caro nodded. "The maids have been drawing straws. No one wants to go into her room willingly. I believe someone is offering their half day off in exchange for not *serving time* with her. Other than that, there has been nothing said about Miss Clara Ashwood and Lady Stafford. Do you think there is any truth to the rumors?"

"Clara Ashwood's appearance in a red gown managed to stoke the fire but I believe she only wanted to taunt Lady Stafford." Which made Evie wonder why the actress would go to such lengths? Any other person might have tried to play it down. Instead, Clara had chosen to act in a manner that only succeeded in raising questions. "I'd like to know how it all started."

"If there is any truth to it," Caro said, "at least Lady Stafford should be able to afford a divorce. I'm sorry to say I don't feel any sympathy for her. Divorce is not an option for the average person who has to rely on abandonment, bigamy or arsenic." Caro tilted her head in thought. "I wonder which one I would choose?"

Evie laughed. Her maid had quite a talent for making light of serious subjects.

A knock at the door was followed by Millicent's entrance.

Caro and Evie stared at the tray she carried.

"On your way somewhere, are you?" Caro asked the lady's maid.

"Oh… Well…" Millicent gave them a cheerful smile. "I thought I might bring in her ladyship's tea, but I see you have already seen to it."

"Millicent, are you all right?" Evie asked. Everyone at

Halton House knew Caro always took charge of bringing in her breakfast but only if Evie rang for it.

"Why are there two cups?" Caro asked.

Millicent's cheeks colored. "I actually thought you might like a cup of tea since you rushed around so much this morning, you might have forgotten. You know, breakfast is the most important meal of the day."

"Are you daft?" Caro burst out.

Millicent lifted her chin.

"Millicent. Please set the tray down and you can each pour yourselves some tea," Evie invited. "And you might as well pull up a chair. I'm getting a sore neck looking up at you both."

"If you insist, milady." Millicent and Caro exchanged a look that brought them one step closer to locking horns.

Caro snorted. "I daresay, if the dowager learns of this, she will have something to say."

Millicent set the tray down and glanced at Caro.

"Oh, would you like me to get the chairs?" Caro asked, her tone mocking.

"How kind," Millicent said.

When they both settled down beside her bed, Evie asked, "Is there something worrying you, Millicent?" Evie couldn't think of any other reason for this uncharacteristic behavior. Taking a sip of coffee, she remembered Edgar's infatuation with Clara Ashwood. Oh, dear, she thought. Had Millicent found out about Edgar keeping vigil?

"Thank you for asking, milady. As a matter of fact, yes there is something wrong. Last night, Miss Ashwood rang for a maid. One of the maids took care of it only to be told

Miss Ashwood wished to have her night cup brought up by Edgar."

Caro and Evie exchanged a brief look of concern.

"Miss Ashwood then proceeded to tell Edgar about her uneasiness," Millicent continued. "She felt Lady Stafford might take it upon herself to pay her a visit in the middle of the night." Millicent took a quick sip of her tea. "And then…" She rolled her eyes. "You would not believe what she did next."

Caro and Evie leaned in, their eyes slightly widened. "What did she do?" they both asked.

"She asked Edgar to read lines with her." Millicent gave a stiff nod. "Right there in her room." Millicent's voice hitched. "And he complied."

"Oh, Millicent. You know Edgar would never do anything inappropriate," Evie assured her.

"I know that and you both know that, but everyone else seems to think he is ready to run off with the actress."

"Everyone? Who?"

"The footmen."

Evie relaxed. "They're bound to jest. You know what they're like."

"Well, it's just not right."

"What's come over you?" Caro demanded. "Only yesterday I praised the way you had maintained your professionalism and look at you today."

"Caro," Evie said, "the circumstances have changed."

"Fine, I'll have a word with the footmen," Caro offered.

"Now I feel silly for telling you," Millicent whispered. "And Caro will no doubt tell me off for barging in here the way I did."

"Nonsense. Caro understands." Evie turned to her. "Don't you, Caro?"

"Of course, milady. Although…"

Evie gave a small shake of her head to discourage Caro from saying anything that might upset Millicent.

"Yes, of course. Millicent should always feel free to come to you with any problem she has." Caro grinned. "No matter how small."

"Of course, she should always feel free to come to me. Now, if you are feeling better I would like to get dressed. Who knows what awaits me today."

Millicent took the tray, bobbed a curtsy and left.

When the door shut, Caro shook her head. "You are far too lenient with her, milady. If you are not careful, your servants will run amuck."

Evie managed to suppress her smile. "Really?"

Caro turned her attention to selecting a gown. "Yes, indeed. She takes far too many liberties. I mean, what was she thinking? Coming in here with such a silly tale and bringing a tray. Despite what you might say, I will have a word with her and she will no doubt come running back to you with her petty grievances. I hope you realize this sort of nonsense would not happen in any other household."

"Oh, really?" And yet, Evie thought, she had heard even wilder stories about some ladies and their maids. In fact, recently she had heard Lord Astor eavesdropped on Lady Astor and her maid's altercations for the sheer amusement of it all.

"No, indeed," Caro said and brought out a green dress only to return it and exchange it for a light pink gown.

"I liked the green one," Evie said.

Employing a no-nonsense tone, Caro said, "You wore green the day before yesterday, milady. Today, you will wear pink."

Evie didn't bother arguing. As for her tolerance… In reality, she knew some of her friends treated their maids like family and it wasn't unusual for some lady's maids to travel first class and enjoy prime accommodation in hotels.

Sighing, she looked toward the window. "The Devonshires have been known to entertain hundreds of people at a time at Chatsworth and I don't remember sensing any type of disharmony among the guests."

"I can't imagine the Duchess trying to run over any of her guests either," Caro murmured. "In fact, I can't even picture her driving a motor car."

"I hope you are not suggesting I have set the tone for this house party." Evie pushed out a breath. "One more day. I think we shouldn't have any problem surviving it."

Evie thought she heard Caro say, "It only takes one moment of carelessness. A devious mind could do a great deal with that."

Evie flung the bed covers off. "That reminds me, I need to telephone Phillipa. Although, I still can't believe there is bad blood between the two women. Lady Stafford knows I organized tickets for everyone to attend opening night. When I told her, she expressed her gratitude and delight. That's not the sort of reaction one would get from someone holding a grudge."

Caro suggested, "Perhaps she was being polite but she secretly writhed at the idea of paying homage to the woman responsible for breaking up her marriage."

"You know about that?"

Caro nodded. "Everyone does."

Evie considered the possibility and then shook her head. "I've known Helen Stafford for a long time and would have picked up on any insincerity."

The sound of hurried footsteps had them both turning toward the door.

A quick knock was followed by Millicent's entrance. "Begging your pardon, milady."

Millicent's cheeks were flushed and she looked out of breath.

"Has something happened?" Evie asked.

"It's Miss Clara Ashwood."

Evie's legs wobbled slightly. She curled her fingers around the bedpost. "What about her, Millicent?"

Millicent scooped in a breath. "She's making her way downstairs as we speak. Her trunks are all packed and she has the footmen carrying them down."

"She's leaving?"

Millicent nodded.

"Without taking her leave?" Caro asked.

Millicent dug inside her pocket and drew out an envelope. "She wrote you a note. She said she didn't think you'd be up and about just yet and didn't wish to bother you."

Evie dressed in record time, all the while muttering under her breath, "This is all going to reflect badly on me, I just know it. I suppose Edgar organized a car to drive her to the train station."

Millicent nodded. "He's running around looking grim-faced."

Caro tsk-tsked. "I don't blame him. Miss Ashwood has proven to be nothing but a nuisance."

Millicent handed Caro a brush and leaned to look out of the window. "The motor car is just driving up to the front door, milady. If you ask me, I think she should have walked to the train station. I don't buy any of that nonsense about being victimized."

With her hair in reasonable order, Evie hurried out of her room, although she had a good mind to wave Miss Ashwood goodbye from her window.

Despite her prompt action, she reached the front steps just in time to see the motor car disappearing down the drive.

Evie huffed out a breath. "Well… Good heavens."

Edgar stood watching the motor car. When he turned, his expression looked downcast. Clearing his throat, he gave a woeful nod. "My lady."

"Don't despair, Edgar. You'll soon be seeing her again." As she turned to go back inside the house, she saw another motor car driving up. "I see the dowager is paying us an early morning visit." No doubt curious to see if anything had transpired during the night, Evie thought.

The motor car stopped and Henrietta hurried out. "Evangeline. I just saw Clara Ashwood driving away."

Evie was about to answer, when a footman rushed out of the house.

What now? Evie thought.

He had a murmured conversation with Edgar who then turned to Evie and said, "Miss Lauren Wilkes and Mr. Wilfred Hartigan have requested to be driven to the train station, my lady."

"Heavens, your guests are deserting you. By all appearances, under their own steam." Henrietta gave her a bright smile. "And still upright. At least that's something."

CHAPTER 6

*A*fter seeing her guests off, Evie and Henrietta made their way to the dining room.

"It looks like we are the first ones down for breakfast," Evie remarked.

"I have already had mine but I suppose I could have some coffee," Henrietta said. "Edgar. You look downcast. You know you should always start the day as you mean to go on."

Knowing the reason for his poor spirits, Evie asked, "How did Miss Clara Ashwood look this morning?"

"She seemed to be in fine spirits, my lady. She asked me to apologize to you for her early departure. She wished to get to London as soon as possible to resume rehearsals."

"I'm glad to hear she felt well enough to travel." Evie helped herself to some toast and eggs. A moment after she settled at the breakfast table, Tom appeared.

Evie watched him stop at the door and scan the room.

"I think Tom is doing a headcount," Henrietta whispered. "By the way, did you check on your grandmother?"

"Caro assured me everyone made it through the night..." Evie shook her head. "She should be down momentarily."

"Well, I'll believe it when I see it." Brightening, Henrietta smiled at Tom. "Good morning, Tom. I see you chose to spend the night at your manor house." She leaned forward and lowered her voice, "Or did you only pretend to leave? I sometimes have the oddest feeling you are lurking around keeping an eye on the place. Then again, you might be prone to sleepwalking. My great-uncle used to sleepwalk. Always the gentleman, he actually took the trouble to dress in his regimental uniform."

"I left late and here I am, in time for breakfast, Henrietta." The edge of Tom's lip kicked up. "According to the footman I just spoke with you are missing a few guests, Countess."

Evie heard Henrietta hum under her breath. "Is that a new moniker for you, Evangeline?"

"Yes, at this rate, I am afraid I might answer to a whistle call." Evie smiled at Tom. "Some of my guests have decided to leave early. At this stage, I can only assume I bored them into an early departure."

Lauren Wilkes and Wilfred Hartigan had both given her flimsy excuses for leaving early, saying they had appointments they had only now remembered.

"Evangeline, you might want to wait until the others join us to make a formal announcement and explain the mass exodus," Henrietta suggested.

"It's hardly that, Henrietta. We must believe Clara

Ashwood was eager to return to London because she wished to resume her rehearsals for the play. The others had legitimate reasons. If you're not satisfied, you can prod for more information when we go to London where we'll see them again."

"If you ask me, it all looks rather suspicious," Henrietta said. "Ah, here's Virginia. I'm sure she'll agree."

"Good morning everyone."

Evie cleared her throat. "I wonder if you would all do me the favor of going along with whatever I say. Martin Gate should be down shortly and I would prefer it if none of this makes the front-page news of his paper."

"I seem to have missed a major part of the conversation," Toodles said as she helped herself to breakfast.

When Evie told her about Clara Ashwood and the others leaving early, Toodles smiled at Edgar. "You must be devastated, Edgar."

"She will be sorely missed... Toodles."

Her granny turned to Henrietta. "There you go. Edgar has no trouble calling me Toodles. How about you try it, Henrietta."

"Oh, my dear Virginia. Edgar is quite the thespian. He's equipped with a certain flexibility I seem to lack."

The newspaper owner, Martin Gate, entered, and gave everyone a cheerful greeting.

"Mr. Gate," Toodles said. "You must be eager to get back to your newspaper and round up the season with a robust bit of gossiping or do you subscribe to different standards?"

Evie sighed and looked heavenward. So much for trying to take control of the situation.

Martin Gate laughed. "That would certainly sell newspapers, Toodles."

"So you don't shy away from a bit of sensationalism."

Taking a seat next to Toodles, he said, "Actually, I tend to find a middle ground."

"That is bound to confuse readers."

"On the contrary. Everyone gets something. Those who prefer sensationalism but don't wish others to know, can pretend they only get my paper for the serious news and vice versa."

"Let me guess. You model your paper on *The Times*."

"You seem to disapprove."

"Well, it's no wonder your circulation is down. How on earth do you expect to sell newspapers if you don't give people what they really want to read? Absolutely everyone loves gossip."

Henrietta gave her an indulgent smile. "I thought newspapers were meant to deliver news."

"Newsworthy events, Henrietta," Toodles declared. "There is a difference. Readers enjoy the unexpected. If a dog bites a man it is not news, but if a man bites a dog, then you have something to engage the readers and they will eat it up."

"We do run a few stories along those lines," Martin Gate said, "but only if we can verify our sources."

"What about if a well-known stage actress has a catfight with a titled lady?" Toodles asked.

Martin Gate's eyebrows lifted. "That sounds intriguing."

"Yes, indeed. Would it get a spotlight in your paper?"

"I'm afraid I would need to be tactful or risk being

sued for libel. Without using specific names, it would hardly be of much interest."

Undeterred by the argument, Toodles said, "They're the best articles. They get everyone talking, especially when the protagonists are disguised by initials. Lady S. and so on. I had a look through the newspapers this morning. The *Daily Mail* grabbed my attention. I guess that's not the one you own."

"No, I'm afraid not."

"They're offering a thousand pounds in prizes for whoever can make the best sand-design advertising the *Daily Mail* on the seashore. I call that enterprising. I hear the masses have descended on the seashore and I'm willing to bet they are all reading the *Daily Mail*." Toodles turned to Evie. "You were recently by the seaside. Were there many people?"

"Yes, as you said, masses of them."

"There has been quite a scramble to make up for the last few years," Martin Gate said. "The numbers have been so great, sofas in living rooms and temporary beds in bathrooms have been snatched up. The police, in some cases, have allowed women and children to occupy cells at police stations."

"And did you run a story on that?" Toodles asked.

He grinned. "Yes. Most papers picked up the story."

Toodles leaned forward and lowered her voice, "So, are you going to run a story on Miss Clara Ashwood and Lady Stafford?"

Evie held her breath.

"I would hate to add fuel to that particular scandal."

Satisfied, Toodles said, "I see. So there is a scandal. I wonder if there will now be a divorce."

How had Toodles heard about that?

Henrietta nearly choked on her coffee.

"Oh, don't look so horrified, Henrietta. You know, we all felt the same way back home until the mid 1890s. Mrs. Caroline Astor had been adamant about refusing to receive divorced persons." Toodles brightened. "And then, would you believe it? Her daughter divorced."

"You misunderstood my reaction, Virginia. I expressed surprise over your assumption there will be a divorce."

Toodles laughed. "Oh, heavens. I forgot. There is a tendency here to avoid making a fuss. Ladies overlook the distractions indulged by some husbands. In particular, those husbands wearing a crown."

Henrietta lifted her chin. "We do not speak of such matters."

Toodles laughed. "We thrive on it back home. Why do you think Lillie Langtry enjoyed such success in America? Everyone wanted to see the Prince's mistress on the stage."

A footman entered and had a murmured conversation with Edgar.

"I have a bad feeling about this, Evangeline."

When Edgar cleared his throat, Evie readied herself for more bad news. "What is it, Edgar?"

"It's Lady Stafford, my lady. She has requested the motor car."

"I take it she wishes to be driven to the railway station?"

Edgar nodded.

"That leaves Horace Gibbins and Lady Manners," Evie murmured.

Edgar cleared his throat again. "The theater critic is already waiting by the front door, my lady."

Lady Manners entered and helped herself to breakfast. "Heavens," she exclaimed when she sat down. She then looked from one person to the other and laughed. "Do I have something on my nose? You all look surprised to see me."

~

"Where are we going?" Tom asked.

"To speak with George Mills about the roses. I'm hoping he might have heard about vandals in the vicinity because the alternative is to believe someone wanted to upset Clara Ashwood by destroying the roses she loves."

"Someone might have been trying to send her a message. Is that what you're thinking?"

Not until now, Evie thought. Hurrying her step, she saw the stables coming into view and her gardener, George Mills, emerging from a side door with a wheelbarrow.

"You're not wearing a hat," Tom remarked. "Hasn't Caro warned you about getting freckles on your nose?"

Evie groaned under her breath. "I'm going to pretend you are all trying to cheer me up." Exasperated, Evie hurried ahead to greet the gardener.

When asked about the roses, George Mills said, "I was just heading over there now."

"Were all the rose bushes damaged?" Evie asked as they made their way along the path.

"No, my lady, just the buds ready to bloom within the next couple of days."

So, the situation wasn't as dire as it had sounded. "I'm glad for you. It was distressing to think your chances of picking up another ribbon had been thwarted by a saboteur. I'm sure the rose bushes will soon recover."

George Mills looked down at the ground.

"Did you discover anything else, George?"

"There were footprints, my lady."

They reached the area which had been set aside for the exclusive cultivation of flowers for the house.

George Mills pointed to the ground around several rose bushes. "I'm the only one who walks around these bushes tending to the plants. As you can see, the footprints differ from mine."

And the footprints were too large to belong to a lady.

When George stepped around a rose bush, Evie looked at the footprints he left behind. She compared them to the other ones. George's footprints were much deeper.

"Tom, walk around a bit… on the soft ground."

Tom looked down at his shiny Oxfords. After a moment, he relented and walked around a rose bush.

His footprints were even deeper than George's. Then again, Tom was taller than George Mills.

Evie returned her attention to the suspicious footprints. They might have been made by a woman wearing men's shoes leaving large footprints but not as deep.

"I'm no expert," George Mills said. "That's why I didn't mention it before. Anyway, the ground has definitely been disturbed."

And now most of the guests had left so Evie didn't really see any point in pursuing the matter. However, while curiosity compelled her to discover the identity of the perpetrator and the reasons behind what might have been nothing but a prank, she suspected there might be a real need to know more.

Evie made a note to ask the housekeeper if the maids had come across any muddy foot tracks around the house.

Turning to Tom, Evie murmured, "What if there is more to this than meets the eye?"

"Cheer up, milady. It's not the end of the world. These days, people have so much on their minds, they put aside trifling matters such as a dull house party. Just because your guests decided to leave early doesn't necessarily mean they didn't enjoy their time here. At least Lady Manners and Mr. Gate are determined to remain until the end."

Both Loulou and Martin Gate had expressed surprise over the others' early departure and neither one had been eager to follow suit. In Martin's case, Evie suspected he simply didn't wish to return to face his dwindling sales… "Is everything packed and ready for tomorrow?" Evie asked.

Caro gave her a whimsical smile. "I see, you are happy to move on. And yes, everything is ready for your departure. Are we all traveling on the same train?"

"No, Tom insists on driving to town. He doesn't like to be without a motor car."

Caro pursed her lips. "I hope you are not thinking of driving."

"What if I am? It would be the perfect opportunity to get some more practice."

"It's… it's not right, milady."

"I don't understand why you disapprove of women driving, Caro. I find it very odd."

"It's just not right," Caro murmured.

"You'll have to do better than that. I won't have you grumbling behind my back."

"Sometimes, I think you forget yourself, milady. You are the Countess of Woodridge."

"Meaning?"

"You have been presented."

Evie's eyes widened with surprise and disbelief. "What does that have to do with me wishing to learn to drive?"

"You more than anyone else know the difference between proper and improper behavior."

"And still, I am none the wiser."

Sighing, Caro explained, "I happen to know why you never ride."

"Would you care to share your insightful information?"

"It's the side saddle. I heard your grandmother mention how much you used to enjoy riding before you came here and I put two and two together. You have never ridden a side saddle and you don't wish to ride astride because you know your peers would frown upon it. Think of all the peers who will disapprove of you driving your own motor car."

"Times are changing, Caro." Evie turned her attention to removing her earrings. "I'll be glad to put this weekend behind me." Although, she would be seeing all her guests in town for Phillipa's opening night. She had already made plans for an after-party at the theater and thought that would be the ideal time to ensure everyone walked away with a positive impression of her.

Hearing the approach of hurried steps along the hall-way, Evie turned toward the door.

"What's happened?" Caro asked as she opened the door to a footman.

Catching his breath, he said, "It's Miss Phillipa on the telephone for her ladyship."

CHAPTER 7

*E*vie tapped her finger on the steering wheel and glowered at Tom. "The sun has come up. Can we leave now?" Not waiting for his response, she put the motor car into gear.

Tom jumped into the passenger seat, adjusted his cap and gave her a nod. "I'm as ready as I will ever be. As the dowager would say, tally-ho."

"What? No last-minute instructions?"

"You'll be driving as far as the village. It's a straight road... more or less. Everyone who is in their right mind is still in bed. What can go wrong?"

Evie pressed her foot on the pedal and the motor car jolted into motion. A second later, she heard Caro calling out at the top of her voice.

"Milady! What in heaven's name are you doing? *You have been presented!*"

Evie laughed and went even faster.

"What does that mean?" Tom asked as he grabbed hold of his cap.

"Caro has the strangest notion about what is proper behavior and what isn't. She thinks driving is undignified. In her mind, I have been presented and must therefore act accordingly. Formal and decorous."

"I'm still lost."

"Rules, my dear Mr. Winchester. There are many but they really only apply to the inner circle and to those with social links to royalty. There are acceptable modes of behavior and routines one must adhere to. The rules include where one goes, what one does..."

"And you feel above it all?"

Evie tipped her head back. Smiling, she sped past the gatehouse. "How am I doing so far?" When he didn't answer, she glanced at Tom and laughed. "If you want to talk, you'll have to unlock your jaw."

"Well, the pillars are still standing, but it was a close call. Actually, you're doing splendidly." He leaned in closer. "At the risk of distracting you, would you mind telling me why Phillipa needs you in town right now?"

When Evie had telephoned Tom the previous night to let him know they would be leaving earlier than planned, she had left out all the details concerning Phillipa's suspicions because they had sounded too far-fetched.

Her playwright friend had become convinced someone was trying to sabotage her play. Her concerns had struck a chord with Evie who had no trouble thinking someone had tried to sabotage her house party.

"She needs my support. This is her debut play and she's worried something will go wrong."

"Is there something you are not telling me?"

"Why do you ask?" Or rather, Evie thought, what had given her away?

"You abandoned your guests."

"I did no such thing. The dowagers and my granny are at hand. Besides, they will all be catching the early train to London and will no doubt arrive before we do."

"And you are still not telling me why Phillipa telephoned you in the middle of the night and urged you to set off for London at the crack of dawn."

Evie recalled the conversation she'd had with Phillipa who'd at least been relieved by Clara Ashwood's safe arrival. The thespian had made her way to the theater and had insisted on jumping straight into rehearsals. Everything had gone on swimmingly and then...

"Clara Ashwood suffered a fainting spell. Phillipa is actually beside herself with worry. There, are you happy?"

The actress had looked perfectly fine when she had left Halton House the previous day and the doctor had given her a clean bill of health. What could have happened to make her ill again? Evie's fingers tightened around the steering wheel.

"We're approaching the village," Tom said. "Perhaps I should take over."

"Someone knows something and they are waiting for something to happen." Evie frowned at her cryptic remark. "Actually, everyone knows what is going on, except us. Most of the guests chose to leave so they could follow the events as they unraveled and secure front row seats to the final scene." In the same breath, Evie said, "Did you know Toodles wants me to do something exceptional? While Caro wishes me to behave more like a Countess. I don't think she realizes that would involve giving her notice and replacing her with a lady's maid who actually knows her place." She scooped in a breath and finished her rambling by saying, "And, now that I think about it, if someone has a problem with Clara Ashwood, I do wish they would have taken action elsewhere instead of at Halton House."

"Countess? Are you all right?"

"Perfectly fine," Evie said in a tight voice.

"I think you should let me do the driving now."

Evie lifted her chin. "No, not just yet."

Evie sat in the passenger seat, her eyes closed, her lips curved into a smile of blissful satisfaction.

She felt the motor car slowing down and heard Tom grumbling under his breath much as he had been doing since they had left the countryside behind and he had begun to weave his way through the London streets.

"I don't suppose you'd care to take over the driving now?" Tom asked. "If you do, I'm sure you'll make the afternoon's edition of some paper or other. The Countess of Woodridge blazed through the streets of London and it has been reported she did the same in the small village of Woodridge where she startled the local Vicar to such an extent, he lost control of his bicycle and ended up in a ditch."

Evie laughed. "I look forward to his sermon next Sunday."

"I still don't know what possessed you to roar through the village the way you did."

"In my defense," Evie said, "I did not expect the vicar to be out and about so early." Shrugging, she added, "In truth, I have no idea what came over me. Perhaps I wished to release some of my frustration. The house party didn't quite go as expected and... Well, I'm sure by the time we return my attempt on the Vicar's life will be old news."

When they arrived at her Mayfair house, Evie wasn't at all surprised to find Edgar opening the front door.

"Edgar, did everyone get off all right?"

"Yes, my lady. Toodles is currently resting as is the dowager. Lady Sara has stepped out to call on a friend. Mr. Martin Gate and Lady Manners appeared to be in fine spirits when we parted ways at the station and I believe I overheard Mr. Martin Gate inviting Lady Manners to lunch at the Ritz."

Evie nodded. "Mr. Winchester and I are going to get out of our dusty clothes and dash off to the theater. Phillipa is expecting us. We should be back for dinner tonight."

"Very well, my lady."

Evie made her way up the stairs. As she looked up, she saw Caro standing at the top of the stairs glowering.

"Have you been holding the glower since I left Halton House?" Evie asked.

"We met the Vicar at the railway station, milady. He had been seeing a relative off and let me tell you, he is not happy. The poor man is walking with a limp. What possessed you to make an attempt on his life?"

"I believe your remark about being presented might have awakened the rebellious child inside me. You see, my dear Caro, I'm not sure I can live up to your expectations or anyone else's, by that matter."

"Are you experiencing some sort of crisis, milady?"

"I might be." And, Evie thought, it might have started with the dowagers and Toodles making it quite clear Evie should show some interest in Wilfred Hartigan. "Oh, I think I have just had a breakthrough. Unless people wish to end up like Nanny Stevens, they really should stop trying to determine what is good for me."

"I'm afraid I don't follow, milady."

"Never mind, Caro."

With a worried look, Caro preceded her into her bedroom just as Toodles emerged from her room.

"Ah, Birdie. Here you are." Toodles followed Evie into her room and settled on a settee at the foot of her bed to recount her experience on the train while Evie changed.

A moment later, Millicent walked in carrying a couple of Evie's dresses. "I've pressed these for you, milady."

"Thank you, Millicent." Turning to her granny, Evie asked, "Was there something in particular you wanted to talk about, Granny? I'm rather in a hurry."

"Not really. Henrietta and I had a long chat on the train and you know how I get when I'm wound up. I just can't stop talking. However, I am rather curious to know why you have two lady's maids. I'm sure I heard Lady Manners say she was having difficulty getting a new maid."

"Yes, that's been the case for many people in the last year or so. And that's the reason why I'm determined to hold on to my household staff, no matter what. There has been a new trend for some people in service to move on to other enterprising métiers. And they're not being replaced because it seems no one wishes to go into service anymore."

Millicent bobbed a curtsey and smiled. "That is not going to happen with us, milady. I can assure you, Edgar and I are very happy in your employ."

"That's very reassuring, Millicent." Evie turned to Caro who remained silent and, in fact, made a point of pursing her lips.

"I think your other maid has different ideas," Toodles said. "Perhaps I could interest her in a job in America."

"Granny, please don't encourage her. Caro is already up in arms because, in her opinion, I am behaving like a naughty Countess."

"I'm glad to see someone is watching out for you," Toodles offered. "If you are to embark on this new investigating adventure, you must remember to keep a low profile."

Evie pushed out a weary breath. "Grans. I don't wish to disappoint you…"

"Good. I'm hoping to see you in action before I leave."

"In that case, I'm sorry to say, you will be disappointed. I'm afraid the small clash between Clara Ashwood and Lady Stafford is all the excitement you will witness during your visit."

Caro cleared her throat. "Lady Stafford called a half hour ago to collect her ticket for the performance."

"I'm glad to hear that. See Granny? All is well. Peace has been restored."

"All is not well." Phillipa rushed toward Evie, her blonde locks poking out in every direction. "This is going to be a disaster. My career will be over even before it begins."

"Why, what's happened?" Evie asked as she walked into the Drury Lane theater. "Has Clara taken a turn for the worse?"

"No, she appears to be fine. It's that dreadful Horace Gibbins. He came to watch the rehearsal." Phillipa drew her toward the doors to the theater, opened them slightly and pointed toward the front row. "He arrived an hour ago. How am I supposed to do my job with him grumbling every time I give directions?"

"Is he even allowed to be here?"

"Some critics like to preview the shows before the general public. As for his grumbling... That's just bad form. He seems to take exception to anything I say to Clara."

Evie thought she saw him tip his head back. "Is he drinking?"

"Yes, I saw him taking a few nips from a flask."

"You really shouldn't worry. I'm sure he's in love with Clara Ashwood. He's always given her performances glowing reviews."

"That might be the case but what if he hates my play?"

Evie looked over her shoulder and saw Tom making his way inside. He hadn't been pleased about leaving his motor car unattended in Drury Lane. "Did you find someone to keep an eye on your motor car?"

He nodded. "The street urchin I found was a tough negotiator."

"A ginger haired boy?" Phillipa asked.

"Yes."

Smiling, Phillipa said, "That's the theater owner's son. Willie. He must have seen you coming."

"So long as no harm comes to my motor car," he muttered and then asked, "did we arrive in time to rescue you?"

"I honestly don't know what we can do to make sure

Horace Gibbins gives you a glowing review." Evie supposed she could bribe him. "Is there something he might want?"

"I just want a fair review." Phillipa grabbed hold of her arm. "He's coming."

Horace Gibbins gestured to Phillipa. As he took another step, he stumbled and grabbed hold of a seat. At least, he tried to. Missing it, he plunged forward and then struggled to straighten.

Phillipa rushed toward him and they had a murmured conversation. Looking over her shoulder, Phillipa held up a finger as if to call for a moment and then made her way with Horace Gibbins out a side door.

Moments later, she returned. "He asked to have a private word with Clara. She's been taking breaks between scenes." Phillipa wrung her hands together.

"How is the understudy? Has she improved?" Evie asked.

"No. I had to let her go. Luckily, Lauren Wilkes dropped by and suggested reading for the part."

Tom and Evie exchanged a surprised look. The Hollywood star hadn't mentioned anything about being interested in the role. Or had she? Yes, Evie recalled hearing her say she wished to try her hand at stage acting. "I take it she impressed you."

"Absolutely. She's marvelous, but I wouldn't say that within Clara's hearing. Here she comes."

Lauren Wilkes gave them a bright smile. "Lady Woodridge. How lovely to see you again. I should apologize again for leaving early. I didn't say anything at the time, but Clara mentioned the understudy's performance left a lot to be desired. I couldn't help offering myself for the role." Lauren gave her a brisk smile. "Actually, Clara suggested I read for it."

Evie remembered the hacked roses and wondered if the movie star had been harboring any hostility toward Clara. As an actress, she would definitely know how to disguise her feelings. "You've made Phillipa very happy."

"I was just glad of the opportunity." Turning to Phillipa, she said, "I just popped in to check on Clara. She said she's ready for the next scene."

"Will you both join me?" Phillipa asked.

Tom looked over his shoulder.

Phillipa laughed. "You can trust Willie. He knows how to play the role of ruffian. You fell for it."

When they reached the sixth row, Evie stopped. "Tom and I will sit here." As they settled down, Horace Gibbins made his way to the front row.

"What's on your mind, Countess?"

"I was just thinking how lucky Phillipa is to have Lauren Wilkes on hand to take over in case something happens."

"You say that almost as if you expect something to happen."

"Frankly, I'd be surprised if it didn't."

CHAPTER 8

"*C*lara Ashwood sounds out of breath," Evie murmured. "It must be hard work making sure your voice carries all the way to the back rows."

"I have no idea what is going on. Do you?" Tom asked.

"It's the third act. I'm sure it will make sense when we sit through the whole play." Evie tilted her head in thought. Something about the scene looked familiar.

Tom nudged her. "If the theater critic keeps drinking the way he is, we're going to have to carry him out of here."

"Did you notice him drinking so much at Halton House?" Evie asked.

"I doubt I saw anyone without a glass," he said. "By the way, did you notice Toodles has taken to carrying around a flask?"

"Yes, I think it has something to do with prohibition back home. The more you put something out of reach, the more people want it."

They heard the doors creaking open and tentative steps approaching them. Evie and Tom turned around.

"What on earth?"

Toodles waved to them. "There you are," she exclaimed in a hushed whisper which resounded throughout the theater.

Henrietta followed several steps behind looking somewhat sheepish. While Sara brought up the rear!

They all made their way to the seventh row and sat behind Evie and Tom.

"What did we miss?" Toodles asked.

Evie was about to ask what they were doing here when Phillipa sprung to her feet and had a whispered conversation with Clara who appeared to be breaking into a sweat.

"They're rehearsing the third act," Evie said. "What are you all doing here?"

"I didn't want to miss anything. The more Henrietta told me about your detecting adventures, the more I realized something always happens when you go off somewhere. She tried to convince me to sit tight and have another cup of tea but I didn't want to miss the excitement."

Evie looked at Sara.

"Your grandmother can be quite forceful when she wants something. And I happen to agree with her. Something is going to happen. Look, Clara Ashwood is about to fall off that ladder."

When Horace Gibbins swung toward them and shushed them, they all settled back to watch the rehearsals.

Evie frowned. "This looks familiar. I've already said that but I can't put my finger on it."

"It's you, Countess."

"What do you mean?"

"Remember that day I found you dangling off the ladder in the library?"

Oh…

Clara Ashwood screeched. "If anyone catches me dangling off the ladder, I will simply say there is method in my madness."

Tom looked at Evie. "I told you."

"I'm sure I didn't say that. And I certainly did not screech."

"You did." Tom laughed. "Look, this is the part where you reached for the book. Did it never occur to you to move the ladder?"

"I can't believe this. Phillipa has based the character on me." Evie had no reason to be shocked. She'd known Phillipa had planned on setting her play at a house party and had drawn inspiration from her stay at Halton House.

Tom burst out laughing. "That's the part where you plastered yourself against the bookcase."

Then it was Evie's turn to laugh. "Oh, yes. I remember. This is when I dropped the book on your head. The actor looks nothing like you and I'm sure you didn't whimper."

"I most certainly did not."

Turning slightly, she saw the dowagers and Toodles trying to contain their laughter. Clearly, Phillipa had nothing to worry about. At least she would make people laugh.

Evie settled back in her seat to enjoy the rest of the scene. Every now and then, her gaze strayed to Horace Gibbins. He appeared to be held enthralled by Clara's performance. When she spoke, he leaned forward as if afraid of missing something.

Tom grabbed her hand. "Is she swaying on purpose?"

Evie's eyes flew to the stage. Clara Ashwood stood in the middle of the stage, her hand pressed against her forehead. She took a step forward and nearly stumbled.

Phillipa half rose out of her chair.

Clara Ashwood then took another tentative step and they all held their breaths. She looked around her as if suddenly realizing she was on a stage. The male actor hesitated and looked at Phillipa as if seeking direction. When she nodded, he rushed to Clara's side and offered a steadying hand. As he reached her, Clara swayed and swooned into his arms.

"Is that part of the performance?" Henrietta asked.

Evie's gaze dropped to Horace to see his reaction. He leaned forward slightly. Evie was about to look away when she saw him continuing to lean forward.

She grabbed Tom's hand. "I think Horace's drinking has gone to his head."

Horace straightened and for a moment, Evie felt oddly relieved but then he toppled over.

She jumped to her feet. Tom hurried toward the aisle and toward Horace. At the same time, the male actor stumbled back and collapsed onto a sofa with Clara in his arms.

Phillipa rushed to the stage. Glancing sideways, she noticed Horace Gibbins and hesitated.

"Don't worry about him," Evie said. "You go see how Clara is doing."

Tom reached him first. Horace Gibbins had crumbled

to the floor. His face looked pale and his eyes were wide open and not blinking.

Crouching down beside him, Tom eased him onto his back and as he did, the bright red rose from his lapel slipped off and slid to the floor. Feeling for a pulse, Tom shook his head. Evie's legs wobbled. She managed to pull herself together and rushed out to the lobby to see if someone could call for an ambulance.

Moments later, she returned to the auditorium and headed straight for the dowagers and Toodles.

"Is he dead?" Toodles asked.

The dowagers and Toodles had been sensible enough to keep their distance and had remained seated on the seventh row.

"I don't know." Swinging toward the theater doors, Evie saw a couple of uniformed men hurrying inside. She pointed toward the first row. Turning to the others, she said, "Perhaps we should go outside. This could become quite unpleasant."

"Heavens," Henrietta exclaimed. "I wouldn't miss this for the world."

"Do you think he might have just had too much to drink?" Sara asked. "He is on the heavy side. Perhaps Tom couldn't pick up a pulse because of that."

They all looked at the ambulance officers who looked quite grim.

"They're shaking their heads. I guess that answers your question. He must be dead," Henrietta said.

Toodles pressed her hand to her chest. "Is this where you step in and solve the murder?"

"Murder? What murder?" Sara shook her head. "The man drank too much. He must have had a condition."

Tom and Evie stood outside the theater and watched the ambulance drive away.

"What now?" she heard herself ask.

"The usual, I suppose. There'll be a service and everyone who knew him will sing his praises."

"You know very well that is not what I meant."

Tom tipped his hat back. "I suppose someone has to decide how he died so they can fill out the death certificate. Meanwhile, I guess the show must go on."

Evie glanced across the street and only then noticed her chauffeur, Edmonds. Crossing the street, she approached him.

"My lady."

"Edmonds, you've had a full day what with ferrying the guests to the railway station and then driving to London."

"It's quite all right, my lady. I've had a nice break now." He looked down the street.

"You must be wondering who that was." Evie told him what had happened inside the theater. "You drove him to the train station. Did he look unwell?"

"When he walked toward the motor car, he stumbled a couple of times."

"Did you happen to see him drinking?"

"Just before we reached the train station. Lady Stafford wasn't at all impressed. I caught her rolling her eyes."

Evie had forgotten Helen had left at the same time as Horace Gibbins. "Do you know if they managed to catch the same train as Clara Ashwood?"

"I believe so, my lady. I saw the train pulling into the

station just as I was driving away."

Evie looked up and down the street and wondered if she should contact Lady Stafford to ask if she had noticed anything odd about Horace Gibbins. "Thank you, Edmonds. The dowagers and my granny should be ready to leave soon."

She crossed the street, her mind a million miles away.

"How did Edmonds take the news?" Tom asked.

"He didn't say anything."

"I wonder if that is a good sign? Everyone in your immediate circle is becoming accustomed to people dropping dead around you. Actually, now that I think about it, I wouldn't be surprised if he hands in his notice for fear that his turn will come."

"I suppose you too are considering it."

Tom smiled. "Oh, no. I wouldn't dream of deserting you, Countess."

"I should go back in and check on Toodles and the dowagers. They'll want to be kept up to date."

"While you do that, I'm going to have a word with Master Willie."

Evie glanced at Tom's roadster and saw the street urchin lounging against the motor car, his cap tipped back, his hands in his pockets and some sort of stick poking out from the side of his mouth.

"Do you have enough money or do you need me to loan you some? I get the feeling he saw you coming."

Evie returned to the auditorium even though a part of her wished to head in the opposite direction. All the way back to Halton House.

She remembered Henrietta remarking on Horace Gibbins' appearance saying his skin had looked pasty.

Evie thought if she had given it any thought, she might have concluded he spent all his time in theaters and not enough time outdoors. Had he been ill?

She didn't wish to think of the alternative, but there was little she could do to stop herself from entertaining ideas about sabotage and murder.

Inside the theater, she looked toward the stage but could not see Phillipa and assumed she was with Clara Ashwood.

Toodles spotted her and said, "We've been trying to piece together everything we saw. I guess we're trying to make sense of it all." Toodles shook her head in disbelief. "One moment he was sitting down and then he toppled over. I'd been watching him and found it all too odd the way he kept swaying backward and forward."

Phillipa appeared from the side of the stage and made her way down a set of stairs. She looked thoroughly beaten. Her downcast eyes and lowered shoulders gave the impression she had been fighting a losing battle. She stopped in front of the stage, looked up and then began pacing.

Henrietta nudged Evie. "I think you must go to her, Evangeline. We'll sit here and… Well, this will be like watching a play."

Evie scooped in a breath. She had come to lend her support but what could she possibly say to make everything better for Phillipa? "How is Clara?" She knew a doctor had been called in but Evie had decided to stay out of the way and wait for news.

Phillipa stopped her pacing long enough to answer. "She appears to have recovered, but she could relapse at any time."

"At least you have Lauren Wilkes to fall back on."

Phillipa gave a fierce shake of her head. "Something's wrong. I can just feel it in my bones."

"You've had a long day. Take a break from all this and come back to the house with us."

"Opening night is only a few days away." Phillipa buried her fingers in her hair. "Maybe it's this theater. It could be haunted or… or cursed."

Evie didn't know how to react to the suggestion and she had no idea what possessed her to ask, "Would you like me to ask around?"

Phillipa instantly brightened. "Would you? Someone must know something."

"Maybe it's just a run of bad luck."

"Tell that to poor Horace Gibbins. How soon do you think it'll take to determine the cause of death?"

Evie fumbled for an answer. "Well, I suppose there's a lot to consider. His can't be the only death today. This is London and there might be… dare I say it, a backlog."

Phillipa brushed her hands across her face. "What will people think when they hear about it? What if they're afraid to come? My play will be a flop even before it opens. Think about it. This is meant to be a comedy. No one is going to want to laugh for fear of disrespecting Horace Gibbins."

Hoping to catch sight of Tom, Evie looked over her shoulder. "Would it make you feel any better if I contact Detective Inspector O'Neill?"

Phillipa gasped in surprise and disbelief. "Would you do that?" Before Evie could answer, Phillipa threw her arms around her. "Thank you. Thank you. How soon do you think you can contact him?"

hen Tom pulled up outside the Mayfair house, they were met by the sight of Edgar pacing up and down, his hands wringing, his eyebrows drawn down.

"Will you be needing the motor car again, Countess?" Tom asked.

"Let me make a few telephone calls and then I'll let you know." Smiling, she added, "This is Mayfair, Tom. Nothing will happen to your roadster and if it does... Well, I should feel obliged to purchase a replacement. Does that make you feel better?"

He brushed his hand across his chin. "So you're saying it's quite possible something might happen."

"Perhaps Edgar can keep an eye on it. It might help him work off his frustration." Evie climbed out and gave Edgar a cheerful smile. Assuming he had heard something about the incident at the theater, she said, "Edgar, you can relax. Clara Ashwood is perfectly fine."

Edgar looked up as if to send up a silent prayer. "It's a

relief to hear you say so, my lady. Miss Phillipa telephoned a short while ago to say you shouldn't expect her tonight, after all. She then proceeded to tell me about everything that happened at the theater."

"A nasty business. We're still in shock. If anyone needs me, I'll be in the library." Evie didn't give herself a chance to change her mind. Taking her gloves off she hurried into the library and went straight to the telephone. The more information she had at hand, the better equipped she would be to deal with Phillipa. Her friend needed all the assurances she could give her.

"Detective Inspector O'Neill, please." Evie waited for the secretary to identify herself but she had clearly recognized her voice.

"One moment, please."

Evie heard Tom entering the library. Turning, she saw him make himself comfortable on a sofa, his long legs stretched out.

"Lady Woodridge."

Evie opened her mouth to speak but no words came out. She tried to clear her throat and that, at least, alerted the detective to her presence.

"Is there something wrong with your voice, my lady?"

Evie squeaked. Once again, she found herself involved in a death. She tried to reason with herself saying it had been time for Horace Gibbins to leave this earthly plane.

Tom pressed a glass into her hand. Taking a sip, Evie smiled in appreciation and cleared her throat. "Detective. My apologies. I'm experiencing some sort of delayed shock."

"Does that mean you require my assistance?" he asked. "Has something happened?"

"I'm not sure." She gave him a brief summary of the events leading up to the death at the theater and waited for his response.

If a pin had dropped, she would have heard it.

"The theater critic," he finally said.

"That's correct. Phillipa is beside herself with worry. Is there some way to find out the cause of death? The sooner I can tell her he died of natural causes the better she'll feel." There, she'd said it. Evie lowered herself into a chair and drank the rest of the brandy.

"I'll see what I can find out for you."

"I'm staying at the Audley Street house." Evie gave him the details. "North Audley," she added. "We'll be here for the rest of the week."

"That's the street that turns into Baker street," he mused.

"Yes, that's the one."

"Is that irony or coincidence?"

She laughed. "I'll take whichever one gets me into the least amount of trouble." Evie thanked the detective and ended the call with a weary sigh.

"Do you harbor any suspicions?" Tom asked.

Horace Gibbins had died right before their eyes. "It's hard to say if he had been ill. He wasn't exactly the picture of good health." However, she recalled seeing him several times before and he hadn't looked quite as bad. In fact, she remembered his cheeks being rosy…

"Had you known him before he came to stay at Halton House?" Tom asked.

"Yes, I was just thinking about that. I knew him from a distance. That is, I knew who he was but I had never been introduced to him." Evie surged to her feet. "I must speak with Helen." She hadn't had the opportunity to speak with Lady Stafford about the incident with the wine glass. Now would be a good time to get some answers.

"I suppose you'd like me to drive you."

"It's not necessary. She lives nearby and it's a lovely day for a short walk."

Tom stood up. "I guess I'll be stretching my legs."

"You don't have to accompany me."

Tom raised an eyebrow. "What do you think Toodles would say about that?"

"I could tell her I gave you the slip."

"At the risk of sounding like an echo, what do you think Toodles would say about that?"

"Fine. You can come, but don't complain if I grumble along the way. I feel justified."

They walked along Grosvenor Square and turned into Duke street.

"I never asked but I suppose I can guess," Tom said. "This is the equivalent of the Upper East Side."

"Yes and Grosvenor Square is Fifth Avenue. Although, I doubt any of these buildings will ever be torn down." As they neared Lady Stafford's house, Evie saw a man standing at the door. He carried a large parcel, which he handed over to the butler before turning and leaving.

"What if Helen Stafford is not receiving visitors?" Tom asked.

"Helen is always at home in the afternoon. She'll see me."

To her relief, they were shown through to the drawing room. And… to Evie's surprise, Helen had company.

"Henrietta!" she exclaimed.

"I'm not sure how to interpret your surprise, Evangeline. Sara is here as is… Toodles."

Evie's eyebrows shot upward. Toodles?

Her granny smiled at her. "Sharing a horrendous experience has brought down the barriers."

Yes, but what were they all doing here?

"Ah, here she comes," Henrietta said and gestured toward the door.

Evie stepped aside to allow Helen to enter. She was all smiles and looked resplendent in a pale blue evening gown.

"Oh, hello," Helen said and twirled around. "What do you think of my new gown?"

"It's absolutely divine."

"Straight from Paris. You'll have to excuse the creases. I only just took possession of it. I know what you must be thinking. I've spent the last few days bemoaning my strained circumstances. Henry is being very annoying. He insists on cutting back on extravagances. But I showed him. There are ways around not having any ready funds."

There were?

"Helen has been telling us of her new venture," Henrietta said. "She has struck up a deal to wear these beautiful gowns to all the right places. She's become a walking advertisement. Isn't it wonderfully enterprising?"

"I didn't want to mention it in case the deal fell through but the parcel was delivered just now." Helen clapped her hands. "And there are more on the way."

Sara came to stand next to Evie and murmured, "We haven't had the opportunity to tell her about Horace Gibbins. Would you like to break the news to her?"

"Well, that's enough showing off." Helen excused herself.

Evie turned to the meddlesome trio. "What are you all doing here?"

"We were on our way back to the house when we saw Helen returning home so we thought we'd stop by and break the news to her but we found her in a flurry of excitement. She had been expecting that parcel and wouldn't stop talking about it," Sara said. "What are you doing here?"

"Oh… the same reason. I thought it would be best if she heard the news from me before reading about it in the papers." She supposed she would have to postpone broaching the other subject of the wine glass. Unless… "You must all be exhausted."

Toodles nudged Henrietta. "That's Birdie's subtle way of suggesting we leave."

"Oh, we can't leave now," Henrietta said. "If we do, I would be as disappointed as last year's debutantes." Seeing Toodles' blank expression, Henrietta went on to explain debutante presentations at court had been postponed during the war and the previous year there had been a huge backlog of young ladies wishing to be presented. The numbers had been so great, they'd all had to settle for a Buckingham Palace garden party, so everyone had missed out on the splendor and glamor of a formal presentation. "This year, they omitted the feathers and the full Court dress. I really don't see why they bother."

"Do you hear that, Birdie? Do not disappoint us."

Helen returned, wearing a dazzling cherry red dress and lighting up the room with her brilliant smile, something that had been missing during her stay at Halton House.

"I suppose you're wondering what's come over me. The fact is, the tedium of the pampered life in a country house sometimes left me wondering what to do next. To think, there are designers willing to part with their expensive gowns for nothing on the condition that you wear them during major social events." Helen stopped and looked about the room. "I would have thought you'd all be happy for me."

"Oh, we are," Evie said. "It's just that… We have some rather bad news."

When Evie told her about Horace Gibbins, Helen looked astounded and asked the same questions everyone had been asking.

"We don't know what caused his death," Evie said. "You traveled down with him. Did he complain of anything? Did he look ill?"

Helen gave it some thought and finally said, "No. Although… it's hard to say. These days, he doesn't exactly look healthy. Or rather, he didn't… Oh heavens, this is a shock."

"You don't suppose his death has something to do with your roses, Birdie?"

"What about your roses?" Helen asked.

When Evie told her, Helen once again looked surprised.

"Why would anyone want to do that? Do you suspect one of the guests?"

Toodles laughed. "If Evie suspects anyone, it would have to be you, Lady Stafford."

Of course, her granny was right. However, Evie would have preferred to work around her obvious suspicions.

Helen fidgeted with the hem of her dress and then laughed. "I suppose I deserved that." She drew in a long breath and rolled her eyes. "Yes, there is some friction between us. If you must know... My dearest, Lord Stafford, is having an affair with Clara Ashwood. They have been carrying on since we came up to town. I assume this is Henry's way of dealing with his changed circumstances and I'm prepared to turn a blind eye until he comes to his senses, but there really is only so much one can put up with." She turned to Evie. "I should apologize for airing my dirty laundry at your house party."

Toodles leaned forward. "Does that mean you're responsible for hacking the roses?"

"Certainly not. Why would I do that?"

"Because they're Clara Ashwood's favorite flowers," Toodles said. "Think about it. There are witnesses who will verify your animosity toward the actress. What if Mr. Gibbins' death turns out to be suspicious? I'm no detective, but I'm sure someone will point the finger of suspicion at you."

"Absurd. Why would I want to kill Horace Gibbins?"

Because he always gave Clara Ashwood glowing reviews, Evie thought. She couldn't think of a better way to get to the actress...

"I'm afraid my granny is getting carried away."

"No, I'm not. I'm merely saying what you can't bring yourself to say."

CHAPTER 10

*T*om and Evie made their way back to her Audley Street house on foot and in silence.

Evie had a moment of regret thinking she should have stayed at the house and waited for the inspector's telephone call. He would surely have some news for her by now.

Tom gave a small shake of his head and laughed. "Do you think Lady Stafford will ever speak to you again?"

"I'm sure she's already forgotten about it all. She saw the humor in Toodles' finger pointing. In any case, I have more reason to be offended. People should know better than to behave like a fishwife in somebody's drawing room."

"You almost succeeded in sounding irritated."

Evie pressed her tongue against the inside of her cheek and tried to suppress her smile, to no avail. "In years to come, I will think back and remember my assault on Wilfred Hartigan and Helen emptying the contents of her glass on Clara's dress. I'm not sure I'm cut out to be a society hostess." Over the years, Halton House had opened its doors to hundreds of guests, including royalty. She knew some hostesses excelled at providing the perfect setting for scandal and gossip. She had now managed it without even trying.

Approaching the house, they saw Edmonds wiping down Tom's roadster. "That's bound to make you happy. Would you mind having a word with Edmonds and making discreet inquiries about the passengers he ferried to the railway station? I've already asked him about Horace Gibbins but he might have remembered something."

"I'll be happy to on the condition you postpone having a word with Toodles until I can be present to witness it. I don't want to miss out on the entertainment."

"I'll make sure to give her a public dressing down." Walking past Edgar who held the front door opened for her, she asked, "Any news?"

"Nothing, my lady."

Evie entered the house. Glancing at the clock on the mantle, she wondered what could be taking the detective so long.

"The dowagers arrived a short while ago, my lady," Edgar said. "They are having tea in the conservatory and Toodles is in the library."

"I see her name rolls off the tongue now."

Edgar bowed his head slightly. "Your grandmother is rather refreshing."

"I'll tell her you said so." Evie looked up at the stairs and wished she had the courage to hide in her room but curiosity compelled her to drop in on her granny and make peace with her. Removing her hat, she entered the library where she found Toodles busy at a desk.

Hearing her enter, Toodles swung around on her chair. "Ah, here you are."

"I see you beat us back and now you are in the middle of something, perhaps I should come back later."

"Wait. I want you to see what I have."

Evie looked over her granny's shoulder at an all too familiar sight.

"I spoke with your maid, Caro, and she told me how you sometimes write the names of your suspects on paper and spread them out."

"Suspects? We don't have any... because there hasn't been a crime."

Toodles straightened in her chair. "What do you know about Lauren Wilkes?"

The Hollywood movie star? "She had a successful career in Hollywood."

Toodles nodded. "And now she's home and she wishes to have a successful career on the stage, but someone is standing in her way."

"Clara Ashwood is alive and well," Evie reasoned.

"Is she really well? She had a relapse and she didn't look so good today. Something is making her ill." Toodles' eyes brightened with a hint of excitement. "She might be the next victim."

Lauren Wilkes had left Halton House straight after Clara Ashwood. Now she had secured the position of understudy in Phillipa's play.

Coincidence?

Evie studied the piece of paper on the desk. Toodles

had written Horace Gibbins' name on the top and had made a list of reasons someone would want to kill him.

To get him out of the way?

Revenge?

On the bottom, a single word stood out.

Poison.

"In case I haven't told you before, your grandmother is lovely," Caro said. "Do you think she is serious about her offer to take me to America with her?"

Evie dropped an earring and bent down to retrieve it at the same time as Caro reached for it. Their heads knocked together and they both sprung back.

Caro grimaced. "You have a hard head, milady."

Evie rubbed her head. "I'm willing to bet yours is thicker than mine."

"In future," Caro said, "please assume I will bend down to pick up something you've dropped. Sometimes I wonder if you forget yourself."

Evie smiled and asked, "Would you be happier if I take a whip to you?"

"I'm just saying."

Evie slipped the earring into place. "Out of curiosity, are you likely to accept my granny's offer?"

Caro tilted her head from side to side. "It's nice to have choices. But it also complicates everything. I should accept an offer that is bound to improve my circumstances. If I don't, I risk coming across as lacking ambition. What would you do if you received a proposal from a duke and another proposal from someone like Tom? Which one would you accept?"

Evie sat back and stared at Caro. "Did my granny put you up to it?"

Caro looked away. "She might have and I don't blame her for wanting to know if you have ambitions to improve your life or if you are looking for something else. She happens to think you will once again settle for nothing less than love, but since you have been living here and have been exposed to English society, you might want to aspire to a grander title."

Evie stood up and inspected her dress. "Caro, you are not to accept my granny's offer of a job in America. I forbid it."

"Very well, milady." Caro smiled at her. "Next time, you might want to try a sterner tone."

"Oh, and please don't encourage my granny to think poor Mr. Gibbins was murdered."

"So... which proposal would you accept?"

Millicent rushed into the room and had a whispered conversation with Caro.

"What's wrong?" Evie asked.

"It's Lady Sara. She has changed her mind about her dress and will be wearing blue."

Evie looked at her reflection. "I am not changing out of my blue dress."

"This one will do nicely." Caro held a coral pink dress. "Come on."

"This is such nonsense... That one has a million buttons."

"Just as well you have a lady's maid to do them all up.

You'll have to change your earrings too. I think the coral ones will look lovely. Or perhaps the pearls."

A knock at the door had Evie grumbling. "I refuse to change my dress again.

A footman entered and delivered a note to Evie.

Evie read it twice and groaned.

"Milady? Is everything all right?"

Evie made her way down to the library with Caro trailing behind her.

"Milady, of all the times to take me seriously. Honestly, I did not mean for you to suddenly turn into a snooty Countess who thinks her maid should mind her own business. Remember what my mother always says. A problem shared is a problem halved."

"Caro, you forget yourself." When she entered the library, Evie purposefully left the door open so Caro could follow her in.

"You're going to call the detective."

Evie gave a firm nod. "Yes, I am." She dialed the number and watched Caro nibbling the tip of her thumb. "Inspector. I just received your cryptic message. I have no idea what you mean by saying I will either make or break your career. Would you care to join us for dinner and explain yourself?" When he answered in the affirmative, she disconnected the call.

"That's it?" Caro asked. "Is there a case or isn't there?"

Smiling, Evie swung around. "Caro, how would you like to step into character and play the role of Lady Carolina Thwaites tonight? The detective is joining us for dinner. You might as well hear everything straight from the horse's mouth." Seeing Caro's eyes brighten, Evie said. "Run along and change. I will join the rest of the party."

Moments later, Evie entered the drawing room and accepted a cocktail from Edgar. Standing in the middle of the room, she informed everyone they would be joined by the detective and Lady Carolina Thwaites. Looking at Toodles, she said, "That's my second cousin, twice removed." She left Henrietta to explain the details and moved toward Tom.

"Tom."

"Yes, Countess."

"Who stands to gain the most by murdering Horace Gibbins?"

"Assuming he was murdered… and without knowing anything about his private life, I'd have to say the understudy."

"Which one? Phillipa got rid of one today and replaced her with Lauren Wilkes."

"Do we know how he died?" Tom asked.

"No, not yet."

"If we're going to assume someone killed him, we'd probably show interest in someone who had the most contact with him."

"That would be any number of people. In fact, anyone who spent the weekend at Halton House." Evie tapped her finger on her glass. Lauren Wilkes would love to play the leading role in Phillipa's play. With Clara Ashwood not at her best, Lauren might well have her opportunity. If Horace Gibbins had not died, he might have given Lauren a bad review…

Good heavens.

What if Lauren Wilkes was somehow responsible for making Clara Ashwood ill in order to step into her role?

"Without having all the facts, this could turn into some sort of blind man's buff game," Tom said.

Evie had to agree. They were blindfolded while the culprit hid in plain sight. "Let's hope Horace Gibbins died of natural causes."

CHAPTER 11

"*H*orace Gibbins did not die of natural causes."

Evie tried to blink. A few seconds before, she had been sipping her cocktail, smiling at Lady Carolina Thwaites as Toodles went along with her maid's alter ego by fabricating a history about a family connection to distant cousins named Thwaites. Tom, dressed in his tails, had been tinkling the piano keys and, to her surprise, had ended up playing a light jazz tune. Just as she'd finished her drink, a footman had entered to announce the detective's arrival and his wish to have a private word with Evie.

"The coroner should have more details in the morning," the detective added. "As you know, I would not normally share this information until we can be certain about what we're dealing with but after a preliminary examination the coroner looked concerned enough to justify telling you there might be suspicious circumstances involved."

"And? I feel there's more you are not telling me."

The detective gave it some thought. "That is all for now, my lady."

Evie nodded. "Come in and join us. After what you just said, I think I need another drink." Walking into the drawing room, Evie introduced the detective to Toodles. "Granny will expect you to address her as Toodles so you might as well get used to it." She handed him a drink and settled down with another cocktail.

Detective Inspector O'Neill took a sip of his drink. "Well? Do you have any suspects in mind, my lady?"

Leaning toward Toodles, Henrietta murmured, "This is a good sign. Our esteemed detective is not so easily swayed by Evangeline's suspicions."

"The game is afoot," Toodles said. Digging inside her small beaded bag, she produced a notebook.

"What is that for?" Henrietta asked.

"I wish to keep track of everything that goes on, of course." She looked at Evie. "This detecting business must run in the family."

"My apologies, Lady Woodridge," the detective said. "I didn't mean to jump straight into it."

"I can only name everyone who attended the house party."

"Is there anyone you found acting particularly suspicious?"

"At this stage, I'm reluctant to point the finger at anyone. However..." Evie mentioned the incident with the wine glass. Lowering her voice, she also added, "We have recently been informed of an affair between Clara Ashwood and Lord Stafford. I... I don't know if that is in any way related to Horace's death... I'd hate to think it is."

"Did anyone happen to notice anything unusual about Horace Gibbins?" he asked.

Sitting back, Evie realized she actually had sufficient bits and pieces which might lead to something. She mentioned her chauffeur's observations about Horace losing his balance and how they had seen him stumbling at the theater.

Toodles piped in, "I think I saw him reaching out with his hand as if… Well, almost as if he were trying to wipe the space in front of him." Uncapping her pen, she made a note of what she'd said.

"And you say he'd been drinking."

"A lot," Toodles said. She produced the small flask from her bag as if to illustrate the point.

Edgar waited for a lull in the conversation to announce dinner.

As they moved toward the dining room, Toodles pointed toward Evie and Tom who walked ahead of everyone. "Isn't there supposed to be some sort of order of precedence according to social rank?"

Henrietta smiled. "Yes, indeed, my dear Virginia. But we're prepared to overlook it, otherwise you would be bringing up the rear."

Once everyone took their places, Toodles watched the footmen pouring wine into everyone's glasses and said, "Horace Gibbins might have suffered some sort of alcohol poisoning."

"From overindulging?" Henrietta asked.

"From bad liquor," Toodles said. "It's been mentioned in several articles in newspapers back home."

"Heavens, I'm sure Horace Gibbins imbibed only the best. Unlike you, we are not deprived."

"Unlike me? Oh, you mean prohibition." Toodles nodded. "It has encouraged people to be creative."

"That has created some unfortunate problems," the detective mused. "The production of wood alcohol is on the rise."

Henrietta looked mystified. "What on earth is that?"

"It's alcohol distilled from wood," Toodles explained.

"How odd. Why would anyone want to imbibe such a product?"

"It's called lack, Henrietta. There are those who can't even afford a potato peel, let alone corn, rye or wheat."

"I take it those are used to produce alcoholic beverages," Henrietta remarked. "You seem to be quite knowledgeable on the subject."

Toodles smiled across the table at Evie and winked. "Let's just say there have been one or two homemade distilleries hidden in our backwoods. There's something about the forbidden aspect of it that draws some men to it."

Henrietta took a sip of her wine. "I take it this wood alcohol you mentioned is quite bad."

The detective cleared his throat. "It can be fatal. There is a toxicologist making quite a name for himself in America. The coroner informed me today he has already evaluated fifty-eight different methods for identifying wood alcohol poison."

"Intriguing," Henrietta said. "But wouldn't one whiff of his breath be enough to determine if he has succumbed to it? This wood alcohol sounds quite unpalatable."

Toodles laughed. "The man is dead, Henrietta. That means he's no longer breathing."

"One of the symptoms is loss of sight," the detective said. "That is something else that cannot be tested now. There's also a sudden sense of weakness, nausea and severe abdominal pain. A lack of coordination and confusion. Some victims slip into unconsciousness and die of heart failure."

Everyone set their forks down. One by one, they picked up their glasses of wine, only to hesitate.

Evie looked at Tom and murmured, "Horace did stumble around quite a bit. Do you suppose his sight had already been impaired?"

"What was that, Birdie? I missed it." Toodles retrieved her notebook and got her pen ready.

"It's only guesswork, Granny."

"I'm sure the detective would appreciate any input that might help him solve this case."

Evie refrained from stating the obvious. They would have to wait until morning to find out if they even had a case to pursue. "Let's assume he had succumbed to the effects of… What is that beverage called?"

"It's actually referred to as methyl alcohol," the detective said. "It is so poisonous, you only need a small amount to kill you. The toxicologist I mentioned warned, even as far back as 1918, of the imminent rise in cases of methyl alcohol poisoning."

Henrietta didn't sound convinced. "Why would someone like Horace Gibbins drink a poor-quality drink?"

"Now that I think about it," Toodles said, "I've heard stories about low quality spirits being mixed with fruit juice to mask the taste. Perhaps he didn't know."

Evie set her glass down.

What if the poisonous alcohol had been mixed with good quality whisky?

"I think Birdie just came up with an idea," Toodles remarked.

Evie shared her suspicion. Turning her attention to her food, she tried to think who might go to such lengths and how they might have achieved it.

"To think I gave up a night at the opera for this," Sara murmured.

Toodles turned to her. "Don't you find it intriguing?"

"Not in the least."

Toodles smiled. "Well, then... Let's talk about something else."

Everyone exchanged glances.

Henrietta cleared her throat. "I hear there is to be a polar expedition soon."

No one seemed to have anything to say on the subject.

Sara looked at Evie. "Oh, do please hurry up and solve the mystery." She took a sip of wine and smiled. "Yes, very well. I am curious. What could have led someone to provide Mr. Gibbins with poisoned alcohol?"

"We are getting ahead of ourselves, my lady," the detective said.

"Yes, yes," Sara agreed. "But no one seems inclined to talk about the polar expedition so we might as well deal with the subject on everyone's mind."

"Is wood alcohol available in our shores?" Henrietta asked.

"It shouldn't be," the detective said. "It's been deemed too toxic for production. Besides, we don't exactly have a scarcity of alcoholic beverages so there is no need for the illegal production of methyl alcohol."

Toodles set her fork down and picked up her pen. "How will you proceed with your investigation, detective?"

"If indeed I have reason to open an investigation, I will be visiting Mr. Gibbins' home and speaking to those in his employ."

"He had a flask on him," Tom said.

The detective nodded. "That should provide us with a strong lead and possibly proof of tampering."

Toodles gasped. "I can't believe someone would put the methyl in his drink. It would have to be someone close to him. Maybe someone who works at his house. Heavens, it might have been one of Evangeline's guests."

Or maybe, Evie thought, someone gave him a bottle of whisky as a gift. It could have come into his possession in any number of ways.

Toodles turned to Caro, "What do you think, Lady Carolina? You've been very quiet."

"Oh, please, call me Carolina. And... I rarely have opinions of my own."

Henrietta hid her smile while Evie lost all control and snorted.

Caro gave her a pointed look, which served as a warning to behave in a more ladylike manner. "In the past, I have been Cousin Evie's sounding board and I have full trust in her ability to come up with a solid lead for the detective."

"I'm sure Birdie can't live without your support. However... I've been thinking," Toodles said, "it's not every day we find a long lost relative. You should come back to America with me and meet the rest of the family."

Caro grinned. "Oh, that would be perfectly lovely."

"Carolina would hate that, Granny," Evie said. "She doesn't care for sea voyages." Did her granny really mean to lure Caro away from her?

"I still don't understand how this methyl could kill someone," Henrietta exclaimed. "Unless someone enlightens me, I will end up tossing and turning all night."

"To put it simply, my lady, it breaks down inside the body and produces formaldehyde and then formic acid. That is what destroys the optic nerve."

"Oh, is that where the phrase blind drunk is derived?" Henrietta asked.

The detective nodded. "Quite possibly. Methyl has been around for a long time."

Evie grabbed Tom's hand.

"What is it?" he asked.

"Clara. She's been stumbling about too." Evie surged to her feet and excused herself to make a telephone call.

Evie set the telephone down. "Phillipa is on her way over to Clara's house. She will make sure she doesn't drink anything she shouldn't. I hope I'm not being overly dramatic."

"Better to be safe than sorry," Tom said.

"I'd like to go to the theater tomorrow morning. Phillipa said she would be there early." Straightening, she shook her head. "I suppose we should rejoin the others. Tomorrow can't come soon enough."

CHAPTER 12

hen Evie entered the breakfast room, Toodles looked up from her sausages and eggs. "Edgar tells us you received a telephone call."

"Begging your pardon, my lady. I didn't mean to…"

"It's quite all right, Edgar." Evie took her time selecting what she would have for breakfast. Taking her place next to her granny, she said, "You are to be congratulated, Granny. After all, you were the first to mention the possibility of poison in Horace Gibbins' drink and then you mentioned the bad liquor."

Her granny's eyes widened. "Are you saying…? What are you saying?"

Evie nodded. "The detective telephoned to say the coroner has found conclusive evidence of wood alcohol poisoning. He actually went into a great deal of detail but I will spare you, at least until we have all had our breakfast." She looked around the table. "Where's Tom?"

"The papers hadn't been delivered, so he went out to get them," Henrietta said.

115

"I doubt there will be anything written about it," Evie mused. "At least, not yet."

Toodles brought out her notebook and made a few notes. "Will you be joining the detective in his investigation?"

"Heavens, no. Why would I do that?"

"If you intend becoming a lady detective, then I would think you'd want to see how the professionals carry out an investigation."

Henrietta laughed. "I believe Evangeline makes up her own rules and that's how she gets results." She tilted her head in thought. "Last night I came to the conclusion a little general knowledge goes a long way. Evangeline is right to congratulate you, Virginia. You did, after all, seed the idea. I'm curious. If it hadn't been wood alcohol, what other idea would you have proposed?"

"Oh, I'm sure there are plenty of ways to get rid of someone. Rat poison comes to mind. There's arsenic in that."

"It makes one wonder how we get on every day," Henrietta mused, "trusting the people who prepare our meals and serve our teas." Henrietta looked up at Edgar who gave her a tight smile. "I am beginning to think I should be kinder to everyone."

"Henrietta. I've never known you to be unkind," Evie remarked.

"Yes, but one never knows. I might say something to offend without even realizing it and then what would happen to me?"

Toodles gave her a bright smile. "Don't you worry about it, Henrietta. We'll make sure to give you a lovely send off and then catch the person responsible."

Henrietta glanced at Edgar again. "I've been meaning to compliment you, Edgar. Everyone in this house is doing a magnificent job."

He inclined his head and then employed a solemn tone to offer, "More tea, my lady?"

"Yes, thank you. There's no point in living in fear."

Toodles set her cup down. "The more I think about it, the more convinced I am Mr. Gibbins received the poisoned liquor in a way that will not be traced back to the killer."

"What makes you say that, Granny?"

"Everyone here knows I brought you a trunk full of magazines. If there had been some residue of poison in the pages, the finger of suspicion would be pointed directly at me. It would be another matter if the magazines had been sent anonymously by post. It's possible Horace Gibbins received a poisoned bottle. It could have been left on front doorstep with no way of tracing the sender... Unless they left fingerprints on the bottle." She nodded. "Will you be assisting the detective this morning?"

Evie laughed. "Granny, I have done my bit, now it is all up to him to bring the killer to justice. Tom and I will be dropping by the theater to lend our support and then... we'll have lunch somewhere. Henrietta has made plans for you and Sara."

Startled, Henrietta glanced at Evie but at her silent urging, she went along. "Oh, yes. Yes, indeed. We'll have tremendous fun, I'm sure. Ah, here's Sara."

Evie took a quick sip of her coffee and stood up. "If you'll excuse me. I need to make some telephone calls. Enjoy your day." Evie hurried out of the room and bumped into Tom, his attention fixed on a newspaper. "Come along. We don't have any time for that." She took hold of his arm and tugged him all the way out of the house. "You get the motor car and I will run upstairs to get my coat and hat. Not a word to anyone." She left him looking utterly perplexed.

Moments later, she tiptoed out of the house and nearly dove into the motor car.

"What's with the rush and secrecy?" Tom asked.

"It's Toodles. She seems to think we're on a case."

"I thought we were. I mean... knowing you."

"Well, of course we are, but I don't want her to know that. Just think of it, they followed us to the theater yesterday. What would the detective say if we suddenly turn up with my granny and the dowagers in tow?"

"The more the merrier?" Tom looked over his shoulder at the house. "I didn't have my breakfast."

"I'm sure you've survived worse."

"Yes, I have and that is the reason why I now enjoy having my breakfast. You see, when you return from a war, you tend to appreciate the little things in life."

"I'll buy you a cup of coffee. Come on, before anyone notices us leaving."

"I guess we're going to the theater."

"No. Make a turn here."

"That's a one-way street and don't you dare say we are going one way."

"Then take the next one. We're going to Kensington."

Tom sighed and gave a knowing smile. "Let me guess. That's where Horace Gibbins lived."

"Yes, Phillipa was very helpful in providing his address."

"You know the police won't let you in."

"We're only going there to observe from a safe distance. We might be lucky and see the detective taking someone into custody. And that will be the end of that."

"In other words, you are praying the killer is someone in his household rather than someone you had staying at your house."

"I really don't see anything wrong with hoping for a positive outcome that will absolve my guests from any wrongdoing."

When they arrived at Horace's house, they sat outside for half an hour before seeing anyone coming out of the elegant house.

Evie reacted by ducking for cover.

Tom laughed. "Do you really think that will work? We're in the only roadster around."

"Knee-jerk reaction." She eased back up and watched the detective standing outside the house talking with one of the constables. After a brief glance their way, he crossed the street.

"Lady Woodridge. Mr. Winchester. It's a nice day for a drive."

"Detective, we won't insult your intelligence by pretending we just happened to be here," Evie said. "We are here because we wish to find out what we can."

Giving a slow shake of his head, the detective said, "According to the housekeeper, shortly after returning from his trip to Halton House, Mr. Gibbins retired to his study to write his column. He received no visitors and spoke to no one. He did not allow any of the staff inside his study. In fact, he kept it locked up."

"There are ways to obtain keys, detective."

SONIA PARIN

"Mr. Gibbins was a generous and kind employer," the detective continued. "His staff adored him and will miss him sorely. Apparently, he had secured an apprenticeship for the cook's son at a newspaper and helped the house-keeper's daughter gain employment as a secretary. The housekeeper is very proud of her daughter's advancement in life and heartily acknowledged Mr. Gibbins' assistance."

"So you are convinced none of the staff are responsi-ble." Yet according to the information conveyed by the detective that morning, the coroner had found the wood alcohol in Mr. Gibbins' flask of whisky. Who'd had the opportunity to put it there? "Did you find any bottles of whisky?"

"Yes, they will be tested. As to where the bottles came from, at no time did Mr. Gibbins receive a gift of a bottle of whisky."

"Perhaps he was given the bottle elsewhere and brought it back with him without the staff noticing."

The detective nodded. "Yes, that is possible." He pushed out a breath, his eyebrows drawn down in frustra-tion. "That only widens the net. We will have to look at all his known associates and friends. Luckily for us, he kept a detailed account of his comings and goings in his appointment book. Including the time he left for the theater the day after he returned from Halton House."

Evie perked up. "Fabulous."

He inspected his notebook. "You mentioned Mr. Martin Gate had been a guest at Halton House."

"Yes. Does his name appear in the appointment book?"

The detective nodded. "Mr. Gibbins met him once a week for lunch at Pinoli's in Wardour Street."

"It sounds familiar," Evie mused.

"It's in Soho."

Evie brightened but refrained from saying the restaurant was on the way to the Covent Garden theater. "So why do you think Mr. Gibbins met the newspaper owner every week? As far as I know, Mr. Gate didn't employ him."

The detective confirmed the fact with a nod. "I will be having a chat with Mr. Gate later today. I hope he will be able to enlighten me." He looked away for a moment, then he added, "There was another name in his appointment book. Lauren Wilkes. He met with her twice since her return to England. Before that, they corresponded regularly during the past year."

"You have the letters?"

He nodded and checked his watch.

Reading his intention, Evie said, "Please feel free to drop by the house tonight. It's an open invitation, detective."

Tipping his hat, he crossed the street and returned to Mr. Gibbins' house.

"An open invitation?" Tom asked. "No strings attached?"

"I really wouldn't want to impose on the detective but I hope he knows I meant for him to bring along the letters. I might be able to read between the lines."

"Because," he prompted.

"Because I'm a woman. That's something I have in common with Lauren Wilkes. Now, drive on, please. I'm feeling peckish. We could stop for an early lunch before going to the theater. I still owe you breakfast."

"And where do you suggest we go to lunch?"

"Pinoli's, of course."

CHAPTER 13

om set the menu down and looked about him. "Pinoli's sounded Italian."

"You should have known what to expect when we walked in. They advertise Parisian dinners on the window. Oh, look, there's *macaroni*," Evie said in a thick Italian accent.

"Yes, *Macaroni au Gratin*. Why not just call it macaroni and cheese?" Shaking his head, he added, "I'm having trouble picturing Horace Gibbins lunching here. I would have thought he'd favor the Ritz, the Savoy or Claridge's."

"I've noticed everyone looking at us."

Tom nodded. "That tells me this is a place only regulars come to."

Evie leaned forward and whispered, "I swear I just saw someone hand over a folded newspaper and the other person remove an envelope from it."

"Are you about to suggest something shifty went on between Martin Gate and Horace Gibbins?"

"Isn't that why we came here? To see for ourselves." Evie hummed. "Blackmail."

Tom sat back. "Intriguing."

"It would give Martin Gate a reason to kill. If you had asked me before today about the relationship between the two men, I would have said they had been in the same room countless times and had never spoken."

"Despite the fact they are both in the same business?" Tom asked.

"Because of that." Evie nodded. "Horace worked for a competitor newspaper."

"They might have been getting together to discuss a job," Tom suggested.

Evie considered the possibility and then shook her head. "Horace's gossipy style would never suit Martin Gate's newspaper." However, according to the detective, they had met here on a regular basis. Why would a black-mailer do that? "Maybe that was Horace's price," she mused out loud. "To force Martin into meeting him in public as a safety precaution. Oh, I do hope the detective will be gracious enough to share more information with us."

Tom excused himself. "I'll be back shortly."

They had been lucky to get a table. The restaurant buzzed with conversation and she could see several people waiting to be seated. When a waiter approached, she told him they were still deciding. However, five minutes later, he came by the table again. The waiter looked desperate to take her order. Tom still hadn't returned. She had no idea what could be holding him up so she went ahead and ordered. When Tom finally returned, she didn't think it would be polite to ask for details. "You're eating macaroni and cheese."

"And what are you having?"

"Chicken en Casserole."

"Shouldn't that be *poulet*?"

"Yes, but it's still listed as chicken. The menu is all a bit of a mishmash. But I'm sure it will be good. After all, Horace ate here and he looked like a gourmand."

Tom glanced around the restaurant. "The detective wasn't wrong about Horace meeting Martin Gate here on a regular basis."

"Did we have reason to doubt the information?"

"No, but it helps to have it confirmed." Tom grinned. "I followed a waiter to the restroom and engaged him in conversation, for a price, of course. As it turns out, Horace rather enjoyed eating here and had made a point of saying it came in handy because it was on the way to the theater."

"I see. That makes sense."

Tom leaned forward and lowered his voice. "Here's something the detective doesn't know yet. Martin Gate always picked up the tab, even when he didn't eat with Horace Gibbins. The meal would just be put on his tab."

Why would Martin Gate pay for meals he hadn't eaten?

"Do you think Horace had something on Martin Gate?" it occurred to ask.

Tom shrugged. "Quite possibly. What other reason could there be?"

"While I like the idea of blackmail, I'm going to guess and say Horace had a healthy bank account and didn't need to use such tactics. He lived in an affluent part of the city. He dressed well. He had regular employment."

"He might have had an addiction to gambling," Tom offered.

"The detective will no doubt look into his finances and I'm sure he'll find nothing wrong with them. Even if he had been blackmailing Martin Gate, I doubt the detective will find a paper trail."

"Having his tab picked up by someone else seems to be small change." Tom picked up the salt shaker and examined it. "If you had something over someone, wouldn't you demand a high price to keep quiet? And if you were being blackmailed, wouldn't you take steps to stop it?"

Evie drummed her fingers on the table. "Martin Gate doesn't strike me as a killer."

Tom smiled. "Because he's too personable?"

"He doesn't take the easy road. His newspaper is experiencing a downturn, something he could improve by giving readers what they get from other newspapers. Instead, he stands by his principles."

As their meals were served, Tom said, "Here's something else I found out. Horace brought Lauren Wilkes here."

"I think we already knew that. Oh, wait… You're right. The detective didn't specify. He only told us they met twice since her return to England but didn't mention where they met." They'd corresponded and had lunched together? What did it mean? "That is a surprise. I don't remember seeing Lauren Wilkes engaging Horace in conversation at Halton House. In fact, if anyone had asked me, I'm sure I would have said they had only just met."

Evie wondered if the detective would allow her to read

the letters he'd found. "I'd like to know why he kept everyone out of his study."

"He either liked things to remain untouched and or unseen by prying eyes," Tom suggested.

If Horace had been blackmailing someone, Evie didn't think he would have put anything in writing.

Tom picked up a fork. "Are we really going to the theater?"

"Yes, I promised Phillipa. Also… I'd like to have a word with Clara Ashwood." She set her fork down. "I actually hope I'm wrong about Martin Gate. Maybe he was trying to entice Horace into going to work for him." She gave him a tight smile. "Yes, I am desperately trying to clear Martin Gate of any wrongdoing and I only have my intuition to go by." She dabbed the edge of her lip with the serviette and surged to her feet. "Come on. We need to get to the theater."

Tom barely managed to get a forkful of macaroni and cheese when Evie grabbed hold of his arm and tugged him along. "I promise to feed you a bountiful afternoon tea."

Arriving at the theater, Evie pointed down the street. "That looks like Lady Manners." Had Loulou been to the theater?

Tom held the passenger door open for her and as he closed it, Willie came rushing out of the theater.

"Same deal?" he asked, wiped his nose with his sleeve and held out his hand.

Tom nodded. "You'll get your money only upon the completion of the task." Tom hurried to catch up with

Evie. "For a moment there I thought he was going to drive up the price."

Evie and Tom found Phillipa huddled in a front row seat going over the script.

"I swear I saw Lady Manners walking away," Evie remarked.

"Oh, yes. She dropped by to see how things were progressing. She couldn't believe Horace had died right here. I told her you'd been here when it all happened so I think she might have been headed over to your house."

"How did she know about Horace?" Evie asked.

"She didn't."

Evie wondered how the young Australian scriptwriter had met Loulou. "I had no idea you knew her."

"We have friends in common." Phillipa shrugged. "Have you heard any more news about Horace?"

Evie related the latest news and watched Phillipa's cheeks redden.

"Martin Gate lunched regularly with Horace?"

"Do you know anything about him that might be helpful?" Evie asked.

Phillipa stared straight ahead, her expression blank. When she snapped out of it, she said, "Sorry, my thoughts were a million miles away…" Phillipa's breath gushed out. "What was the question?"

Evie repeated the question. "You seemed to be surprised at the connection."

"I wonder…" Phillipa tapped her pen against the armrest. "Horace said something a short while ago about funding my next project. He said it would be easy to find the money. It struck me as odd because I've never known him to become financially involved with a play. He was going to wait until this one had its full run before discussing the details."

"Did he happen to mention where the money would come from?"

"No, he only said I had no reason to worry. I ended up having a restless night because I knew there had to be a catch." Phillipa set her script aside. "I guess you don't have any news about ghosts or curses. I was sort of hoping you would."

Had Horace been trying to secure funding for Phillipa's next play? Martin Gate's newspaper might be experiencing poor sales, but he came from a wealthy family.

"Is Clara in her dressing room?" Evie asked.

"Oh, I do hope so." Phillipa groaned. "Sorry, I keep thinking something else will go wrong."

As Evie and Tom went out through a side door, Evie thought she heard her granny calling out to Phillipa. She grabbed hold of Tom's arm and tugged him along. "I knew it. They followed us and now they've caught up with us." Seeing a stagehand, she scribbled a note and asked if he could deliver it to Phillipa.

"Let me guess, you've asked Phillipa to keep Toodles entertained."

"With any luck," Evie said, "we might be able to make our escape without being noticed."

They found Clara Ashwood slumped over her dressing table. Evie thought there seemed to be a lot of that going around. When the thespian didn't move, Evie panicked and shrieked her name, "Clara!"

Clara sprung back and nearly fell off her chair. "Heavens, you nearly startled me to death."

"That would have taken some explaining to Phillipa," Tom murmured.

Rolling her eyes at Tom, Evie said, "I hope you don't mind us barging in on you like this."

Evie didn't want to mention any details about the case for fear it might interfere with the police investigation. She looked around the dressing room and saw a vase of red roses. That's when she noticed the air was thick with the fragrance. Almost to the point of being pungent. "I had no idea roses could have such a strong scent."

Clara tapped a bottle of fragrance. "Oh… I actually spray my dressing room with the scent."

Nodding, Evie sat down on a chair near the door. "You must be devastated by what happened yesterday. Horace was your greatest supporter."

"He will be missed." Clara turned to face the mirror and began working on her hair and make-up. "My apologies. We're having a dress rehearsal this afternoon. You know what they say, the show must go on."

Reluctant to leave without asking any questions, Evie said, "I understand you spoke with Horace several times before… before…"

"Before he keeled over," Clara said. "I guess that sounds insensitive. I'm trying to make light of the matter as a way of coping. After all, he was my most ardent admirer. You know, I often warned him about his health. He should have taken better care."

Had someone identified drinking as his weakness? It would suggest careful planning by the killer. Find the victim's weakness and exploit it, Evie thought.

Evie decided to break her golden rule and filled the

actress in on the latest news. "The police found wood alcohol in his system."

"Wood alcohol? What on earth is that?"

A further explanation yielded an equally astonished response.

"But how? Horace was fond of his whisky and rather particular about it. In fact, his only interest outside of the theater was to visit whisky distilleries. He always spent his vacations in Scotland, touring the distilleries. From what he told me, he'd always return with a hoard."

Evie wanted to allude to the possibility of murder just to see Clara's reaction, but she felt she would be treading on the detective's toes. Although, having mentioned the toxic substance, she felt the actress should have made the connection.

Evie waited for Clara to ask the obvious question about who might want him dead, but she didn't. At least, not straightaway.

Clara looked pensive as she said, "Every day, there's something or other about someone dying under mysterious circumstances." She glanced at Evie. "Do you think someone might have tampered with his whisky?"

"It's a possibility," Evie said.

Clara appeared to give it some thought and then shook her head. "There must be some mistake but if the police are looking at possible enemies, they will have their work cut out for them. Horace left quite a trail of wrecked careers. He felt it was his duty to cleanse the theater of mediocre hacks."

"I suppose you consider yourself lucky. In his eyes, no other actress could come close to matching your talents." Evie didn't detect the slightest hint of modesty. Instead, she thought Clara took the remark as a given. "I know he came to see you during rehearsal breaks… Can I ask what you two talked about?"

Clara gave her a whimsical smile. "He liked to think he knew best. Poor Phillipa, he'd been overriding every single direction she gave me. Lauren Wilkes told me she'd been quaking in her boots. She spent the last few days pampering me and making sure I didn't have another relapsed for fear that she might have to go onstage."

"Are you saying she didn't want your role?"

"Heavens, no. She only did it as a favor to Horace. She has too much pride to become an understudy and prefers to wait until she's given the leading role."

"Why did Horace want her to be the understudy?"

Clara shrugged. "I guess we'll never know."

More than ever, Evie hoped the detective came through and shared the contents of the letters between the silent movie star and Horace Gibbins.

Tom's stomach gave a loud protest.

"My apologies," he said.

"We should leave you to it." Walking out of the dressing room, Evie dug inside her handbag. "Here, have a scotch mint."

"What happened to the bountiful afternoon tea you promised me?"

"It will have to wait. We have to make another stop and… We have to go out the back way."

CHAPTER 14

"*Y*ou didn't ask Clara Ashwood about her affair with Lord Stafford."

"I forgot."

"Forgot?"

"Even if I had remembered, I suppose I would not have felt comfortable prying. Besides, do we really need it confirmed? Lady Stafford didn't make a big deal out of it. She was more interested in her new dress."

"Have you taken Lady Stafford off the list of suspects?" Tom asked.

The thought of Helen killing Horace Gibbins in order to deprive Clara Ashwood of her greatest supporter seemed too far-fetched and complicated to consider. "If Helen had been in any way involved in Horace's death, I doubt she would have volunteered the information about the affair."

Tom disagreed. "It would be the perfect ruse. Put everything out in the open."

Evie closed her eyes and tried to picture Helen plotting Horace's demise. Where would she have obtained the wood alcohol? She supposed it could have been distilled especially for her.

Another thought struck.

Lauren Wilkes had recently returned from America. She could have brought the wood alcohol with her. "What possible reason would Lauren Wilkes have for killing Horace?"

"I thought we were discussing Lady Stafford," Tom said.

"Yes, we were, but then I moved the conversation forward." Evie reached for her hat before it flew off. "What are you doing?" Evie asked as Tom turned into a side street so fast, the motor car tilted and the tires screeched.

He pulled up in front of a car and turned to look over his shoulder. Several seconds later, they saw the Duesenberg drive by.

"You're kidding." Evie straightened. Toodles and the dowagers had followed them from the theater.

"Do you still want to head out to Martin Gate's newspaper?" Tom asked.

"No…" She drew out her notebook and searched for an address. "Let's pay Wilfred Hartigan a visit instead. I only have his home address. If we don't find him there, we should be able to get his business address."

"Will this be a social visit or do you think he might know something?"

"Good question but not one I can actually answer just yet." Moments after Clara Ashwood had left Halton House, Wilfred Hartigan and Lauren Wilkes had followed. And soon after, Horace Gibbins had also left. And they had all met at the railway station. Surely, someone had noticed something.

"They caught the same train. I'm hoping he might have seen something the others missed. You can never tell what might come in useful."

"I think the coast is clear. Where are we going?"

"St. James. Drive along Piccadilly." Evie gave him directions to Wilfred's house. "Even in the open car I can still smell the scent of roses. I think it permeated my clothes." Evie leaned forward and sniffed Tom's sleeve.

"I hope you're not really complaining. You can explain it away, but how can I explain smelling of roses?"

"I guess you'll just have to make sure you stand close to me. Now... What was I saying before?"

"You were hoping Wilfred will crack the case open for you. I've no doubt he will. The moment he sees you, he'll probably cower in a corner and start singing like a canary."

"I'm sure he's already forgotten about those silly incidents. By the way, how do you make the car roar like that? It doesn't seem to do it for me."

Tom shifted gears and overtook a slow vehicle. He laughed. "You want to make it purr, not roar."

Pointing ahead, Evie said, "Turn into that little street."

Tom leaned forward. "Is that the Ritz?"

"Turn or you'll miss it."

"My apologies. Some people are led by their hearts. At the moment, I'm being led by my stomach."

"Would you like another scotch mint?"

"I guess I'll take what I can get. Thank you."

Evie kept her eyes on the house numbers. "That's the house. I hope Wilfred Hartigan is home."

"I'll go up and check," Tom offered. "You stay and look after the roadster."

"Are you sure you have the energy to walk up the steps?" Evie watched him walk up to the smart four-story house. Within a second of lifting the knocker, the door opened and a butler greeted him. Tom returned with a piece of paper in hand.

"He's at the publishing house and we're now headed to Bloomsbury."

"Oh, that's not far. I'm sure we'll find you something to eat there."

As he got the roadster moving, he glanced over his shoulder at the Ritz in the corner, "There was something to eat here."

"You're such a good sport."

"Scotch mints *and* praise. I feel I should wag my tail." He turned into the next street and glanced back toward the Ritz as if to make a point only to laugh. "You won't believe this. The Duesenberg just turned into the street."

"They really are following us. Toodles must have figured out we're going around talking to everyone who attended the house party."

"We are?"

"Yes, we seem to be. Now, step on it. They're bound to catch up."

Tom laughed. "Actually, I took precautions and told the butler not to give out Hartigan's whereabouts."

"That was cunning. What made you think of it?"

"I know Toodles. Although, despite my efforts, I'm sure she'll find a way to get the information out of the butler. She can be persuasive." Tom tipped his hat back and focused on the road. A moment later, he said, "When you say we're talking to everyone, surely you don't mean to do it today."

"Don't worry. We'll head back to the house in time for dinner. The town cook really likes to put on a feast."

Tom snorted. "You really expect me to fall for that carrot again. You've been very generous with your promises, offering sumptuous afternoon teas and dinners... I'm not sure I can trust you."

"I wonder how the detective is getting on." If Toodles and the dowagers couldn't get an address for Wilfred Hartigan, Evie thought they might head over to Martin Gate's newspaper office and... they might bump into the detective. "Oh, what I'd give to see that," she murmured.

"What did you make of Clara Ashwood's response to the news of Horace's death being caused by wood alcohol poison?"

Evie thought she had sounded surprised and hadn't appeared to know anything about the substance. She had remained relatively calm... "I wonder if we witnessed a fine performance?"

"I've been entertaining the same thought."

"We would have to dig deep for a motive. Horace had been her champion." Evie straightened. "Now that I think about it, Clara was rather quick to speak of him in the past tense. Most people need time to adjust."

"She already enjoys a solid reputation. It sounds as if he had made a nuisance of himself by interfering with Phillipa's work." Tom slowed down and made a turn. "It's possible he had outlived his use."

"You think we should consider her as a suspect?" Evie drew out her notebook and wrote down a few reminder notes to herself. She set her pen down and frowned. "Something doesn't make sense."

Tom glanced at her.

"I'm trying to remember something…" She tapped her pen against the notebook. "We saw Lauren Wilkes the first day we went to the theater. She apologized for leaving Halton House early and went on to explain…" This time, she tapped her pen against her forehead. *"I couldn't help offering myself for the role.* Yes, that's what she said right after mentioning Clara had talked about the understudy doing a poor job of it. Oh… Then she said Clara had suggested she read for the part." Evie curled her fingers around Tom's arm. "Yet Clara just told us Lauren Wilkes has no interest in the understudy role."

"Someone's lying?"

"Yes, and the question is why? They're both being deliberately misleading. They might be trying to hide an obvious motive."

"You think they're working together and covering for each other?"

They were up to something. Evie couldn't see any other reason why they would offer contradictory information.

"Here's another question," Evie said. "Why do you think the killer chose the theater?"

"Maybe he or she didn't. If we're actually thinking Horace was sent a bottle of whisky with wood alcohol, the killer must have known he wouldn't be able to control when Horace drunk it."

"I like that," Evie said. "The killer must have been prepared to bide his time."

When they reached the unassuming publishing house

building, Tom looked around. "I suppose there's enough foot traffic here to leave the roadster."

"You've never been concerned about the roadster before."

"You're right. Maybe it has something to do with you using it as a weapon to nearly run over Wilfred Hartigan."

"Thanks for reminding me. I told Caro Wilfred strikes me as someone too sure of himself. He had been getting on my nerves…"

"It's a front," Tom said. "The man is full of insecurities."

"I thought Sara said he'd turned the publishing house around. That's something to be proud of."

"And still, he's insecure. I think it might have something to do with not serving."

"Serving?"

"During the war. He failed his medical."

They walked inside the building and made their way to the top floor office. The place was a beehive of activity with stacks of books on every available surface. A young woman directed them to an office at the far end of a spacious office filled with desks. Large windows acted as a partition and they could see Wilfred leaning against his desk talking to someone.

"Looks like he has company." Drawing closer, Evie saw a woman sitting opposite him on a sofa. "Loulou! We've caught up with her."

Both Wilfred and Loulou looked toward them. At first, they looked uncertain. Lady Manners shifted to the edge of the sofa as if she intended to get up and leave but Wilfred signaled to her. Evie read the gesture as a suggestion that she stay.

If they said anything, she did not hear them through the glass window.

Wilfred opened the door and welcomed them. "Lady Woodridge. Mr. Winchester."

"Evie, please."

"Of course. Come in. Make yourselves comfortable."

Evie smiled at Lady Manners. "Loulou. How lovely to see you. Actually, I'm sure I spotted you near the theater."

Tom shook hands with Wilfred and walked past him to go stand near the window. Evie saw him casting his gaze over Wilfred's desk and wondered if he had seen anything of interest.

"Lady Manners has just been telling me about Horace. I'm surprised it hasn't made the front page of the newspapers."

Loulou nodded. "I just told Wilfred if anyone knows something it will be you, Evie."

Tom cleared his throat. "Unfortunately, Evie is not at liberty to speak."

"Oh, really?" Loulou could not have looked more surprised. "Does that mean you do know something? Yes, of course, it does." She clapped her hands. "Fabulous. Do tell."

"Actually, I wondered if either of you heard Lauren Wilkes talk about the play during the week-end," Evie said.

Loulou sat up. "Does that mean she's involved in Horace's death?"

"I didn't say that." Evie realized she had drifted off toward the deep end. She had already told Clara Ashwood about the wood alcohol. If she continued revealing privileged information, she risked hindering the investigation.

Wilfred smiled. "News of his death didn't make it to the newspapers. That has to mean something. Is the information being suppressed because there's some doubt as to how he died? Yes, that must be the case. Oh, and you are here to find out what you can. Are you collaborating with the police?"

Evie looked at Tom who simply shrugged as if to say he'd already helped her out.

"As Tom said, I am not at liberty to share anything. However, there are suspicious circumstances. Did either of you notice anything unusual during the week-end?"

Loulou laughed. "Your attempts on Wilfred's life were rather unusual. Anyone would think you were trying to cause a diversion."

"Now, there's a thought," Wilfred said.

Evie turned to Loulou. "I've been wondering about the incident with the wine glass."

Loulou shared a knowing smile with Wilfred. "Yes, that was rather entertaining but not surprising."

"Is there something you know?" Evie asked. "You always have the juiciest gossip…"

Loulou winked at her. "Well, it's really not for me to say."

"We visited Lady Stafford," Tom said. "She had some revealing news about the state of… affairs."

Loulou pressed her hand to her throat. "Oh, thank heavens. It's out in the open. I'm hopeless at keeping secrets."

Evie glanced at Tom and found him looking rather pleased with himself.

"So you know," Evie said.

"About the affair?" Loulou nodded. "Yes, everyone

knows. Horace was such a vile creature, he had proof of the affair but he threatened to discredit Lady Stafford in his column all in order to restore Clara Ashwood's reputation."

Really?

"But that would give Lady Stafford reason to…" Evie gasped.

Loulou and Wilfred leaned forward and both said, "Kill Horace Gibbins?"

The young woman who'd shown them through to Wilfred's office knocked on the door. Evie looked up and saw the detective waiting to be announced.

Tom shifted. "I suppose this is our cue to leave."

"Why? What's happened?" Loulou asked and looked around. "Who's that?"

"That's the detective in charge of the investigation," Evie said.

"So there is an investigation." Loulou chortled. "Did you come here to interrogate Wilfred?"

"I only wanted to know if he'd noticed anything… Oh, never mind. We'll see ourselves out."

Evie hurried out of the office and tried to weave her way around the desks so as to avoid the detective but he cut her off.

"Lady Woodridge. Why am not surprised to find you here?"

"Detective. Any news?"

"Yes, your grandmother appears to be hot on your trail. I had just finished my interview with Mr. Martin Gate when she appeared at the door. She wasn't alone. The dowagers were with her as well as Lady Carolina Thwaites."

Caro?

"I hope she didn't cause any disruptions, detective."

"I might take you up on your offer and drop by your house tonight. Your grandmother might have learned something that could come in useful."

"And did you find out anything useful from Martin Gate?" Evie asked.

When the detective answered, he didn't sound at all convinced. "Mr. Gate wanted to get information on his competitor. He struck a deal with Horace Gibbins."

"Lunch at Pinoli's in exchange for information? I find that hard to believe."

"That's as much as I could get out of him…"

Evie took the detective's small nod as a prompt. "Do you wish me to delve?"

"I wouldn't put it into so many words, my lady." The detective tipped his hat. "If you'll excuse me, I'd like to have a word with Mr. Wilfred Hartigan."

As he turned away, Loulou hurried past him undetected.

Evie walked on and caught up with her. "Loulou. I meant to ask, have you found something to engage your interest? I hear you have been doing quite a bit of writing lately." Evie expected her friend to deny it.

"As a matter of fact… I'm writing a memoir. Actually, I started to write one but then I became diverted by the idea of writing a story."

"About what?"

"A murder mystery." Loulou gave her a cheerful wave. "Must be off. I'm meeting one of Phillipa's writer friends for afternoon tea. She's going to give me some pointers."

CHAPTER 15

*E*vie watched her friend, Loulou, turn the corner. A moment later, her pale blue motor car whizzed by. Waving, Evie huffed, "Once again, Halton House has become the inspiration for another murder story. I should charge a fee for anyone staying there."

Tom held the passenger door open for her. "And I should abandon you right here and go chasing after Lady Manners. She's going to have afternoon tea. The woman offers greater prospects. And don't you dare offer me another scotch mint."

Evie settled into her seat and pointed ahead. "I'm sure Martin Gate will have coffee."

"Remind me again why you wish to speak with him."

"The detective isn't satisfied with the information he got from him."

"But you're not on the detective's payroll," Tom reminded her.

"Perhaps I have become a champion for the truth,"

Evie declared. "I believe that is reason enough to forgo an afternoon meal."

"It's three for me," he murmured under his breath.

"I've never known you to complain," Evie murmured back. Digging inside her handbag, she drew out her notebook and made a note to remind herself to contact Halton House and speak to the housekeeper. In her haste, she had forgotten to ask if any of the maids had discovered mud tracks in the house.

She then made another note about whisky. Did Horace have a favorite brand? Had the detective entertained the same thought and organized for all the opened bottles to be tested? Had they looked around the house for signs of someone breaking in?

The detective had said all the servants adored Horace but it wouldn't be the first time someone bit the hand that fed them...

She tapped Tom on the shoulder and leaned in to ask, "If you have a favorite brand of whisky, what would compel you to drink something different?"

"There are always special, rare bottles. That would definitely steer me away from my usual drink."

So they should be looking for something exceptional.

Nearing the newspaper office, they saw people milling about and, for a moment, Evie panicked. Then, she made the connection.

"It's the afternoon edition," Evie said catching sight of a boy waving a newspaper and hollering for attention.

Tom brought the roadster to a stop right outside the building.

They grabbed a copy and stood by reading the front page. "I wonder if any of the other papers are running the story," Evie said as she read the announcement of Horace Gibbins' death.

"Perhaps Martin Gate got the go-ahead from the police to print the exclusive scoop."

"Let's go find out." Evie hurried inside the building only to collide with Martin Gate. "Ah, the man himself. Where are you off to?"

"A late lunch. Care to join me?"

"Yes," Tom said.

"Will it be private enough to talk?" Evie asked.

"It's a rather noisy pub. What did you want to talk about?" Martin clicked his fingers. "That reminds me. Your grandmother came by." He laughed. "She had a note-book in hand and shot off one question after the other. The dowagers were with her and another lady. Let me see, what was her name... oh yes, Lady Carolina Thwaites. She and your grandmother took turns to fire questions. I believe they were trying to trip me up."

"Can we walk and talk?" Tom urged.

"Tom is fading fast," Evie explained, "he hasn't eaten all day."

"I know the feeling. I'd been about to step out when the detective showed up and then your grandmother or was it the other way around? It's been one of those days."

"Is the pub far?" Tom asked.

Evie wove her arm around his. "Just in case you faint from hunger."

They walked out of the building and made their way through the throng of people. Evie checked her watch. "It's rather busy out here."

"It's always like this at this time of day," Martin said as he nodded to a few passers-by.

Evie held up the newspaper. "I see you broke the news."

"Oh, yes… Finally. In fact, I got the exclusive, with the detective's permission, of course."

"Did he ask you to print anything specific?"

"Funny you should ask… He told me I could include the cause of death but he specifically asked me to exclude anything that might suggest Horace had been killed."

"Did he say why?" Evie asked.

"Apparently the higher ups wished to use the incident as a public announcement." He shrugged. "I believe they want it to be read as a warning to anyone thinking of distilling their own alcoholic beverages."

"Could there be another hidden agenda?" The killer now knew the cause of death had been identified. "What would you do if you were the killer?"

Martin laughed. "It's strange to think of myself as a suspect. I'd like to think I had been careful to avoid leaving a trail." He gestured toward the pub. "I hope you don't mind eating at a pub."

"Steak," Tom said. "Sounds good to me."

"I haven't seen steak on the menu in quite a while or anything other than a variety of pies."

They walked past a group of men at the bar and made their way to an enclosed area.

"This should give us some privacy. While you settle down, I'll go have a word with the bartender. It's well past the usual meal time but I'm sure he'll organize something."

The prospect of going without yet another meal had Tom staring blankly at Evie.

Laughing, Evie called out, "For goodness' sake, bring

some bread at least." She patted Tom's hand. "I'm sure he'll manage something. I need you to focus. Somehow, we must find out why he met with Horace every week and why he picked up the tab. Here, have some water."

Martin returned and set a basket of bread rolls on the table. "I don't know about you, but I'm starved. What with all my visitors and with trying to get a late edition out…"

Both men dove for the bread, not even bothering with butter.

"It seems to me the dowagers and Toodles… oh… and Lady Carolina Thwaites felt you had valuable knowledge to share. As it happens, I know the detective wanted to find out why you had lunch with Horace every week."

As Martin chewed he rolled his eyes from side to side. Finally, he said, "It's all nonsense. Cloak and dagger, that's what he made it sound like. As if I would ever become involved with something illicit."

"Perhaps not by choice, but what if you were forced into it? We're thinking Horace had something on you." Evie watched for the slightest hint of complicity but Martin's eyes brimmed with humor. "If they look hard enough, are they likely to find something to link you to his death?" The humor in his eyes remained but Evie had the distinct impression Martin had to put a lot of effort into it.

Their food arrived and seeing how eagerly Tom dug into his pheasant pie, Evie pushed her plate toward his. Smiling, Tom took a bite of his pie, savoring the morsel with reverence.

Evie hit a brick wall and had no idea how to cajole information out of Martin other than by stating the obvious. "We know you gave him *carte blanche* at Pinoli's. The police seem to think he was blackmailing you."

Martin shrugged. "It was nothing but a business arrangement. One word from Horace, and readers would have abandoned my newspaper in droves. The man's influence is… was far-reaching."

"We're not buying that," Tom said. "The Countess and I are bound to spend the evening trying to come up with a reason for your meetings. She has the detective's ear and if she happens to come up with anything of interest, he will pursue it."

Martin laughed. "Are you trying to get me to pick up your tab?"

Evie straightened. "So, he did have something on you."

Martin's cheeks colored slightly. Evie watched him take a deep swallow and try to hide the proof of his discomfort by reaching for his glass of water.

"It was all a game to him," Martin finally said. "He didn't need me to pay for his lunch. But he relished the idea of wielding power over me." He set his glass down and pushed the plate away. "I'm afraid I've lost my appetite."

When he surged to his feet, Evie looked at Tom, her eyes wide with panic. They hadn't heard the whole story.

"If you'll excuse me," Martin said.

"Wait," Evie urged.

Lowering his voice to a whisper, he explained, "This is not something I can talk about in public." Martin Gate turned and rushed out of the pub.

Evie jumped to her feet. "Come on."

"What?" Tom looked down at his pie. He'd only managed one bite.

"Forget the pie. Come on." Evie grabbed his arm and tugged him along. They followed Martin back to his office. Along the way, Evie tried to imagine what his secret might be and came up with nothing. Although…

"An affair?" she mouthed at Tom who shrugged.

Surely it couldn't be an affair. Those were too commonplace to register as a point of interest. Just about everyone she knew had them.

Then again…

Affairs between men were still quite illegal and social taboos.

Surely not.

Martin Gate looked like… Well, a man. Quite masculine. Evie decided she would need to reappraise her preconceived notions since they were mostly based on what she'd seen at exclusive fashion salons were certain men displayed outrageously exaggerated female qualities.

Such a nuisance, she thought. It all seemed like so much hard work to change one's mind and form new opinions.

Martin went straight through to his office, ignoring his secretary when she tried to give him a telephone message.

As Evie and Tom joined him, he drew the curtains and closed the door.

"Well," Evie said as she tried to make light of the matter. "That should be enough to alert everyone there you are in the midst of a secret meeting."

Martin held up a bottle of whisky and gave them a brisk smile. "Drink?"

"Not for me, thank you." Evie sat down.

"Not on an *empty* stomach." Tom declined the offer and sat next to Evie.

"It's an affair," Martin said.

"Why the fuss?" Evie asked, her tone surprised.

He lowered his voice to barely a whisper. "A prominent politician's wife. Heaven help me. I took every care. It never occurred to me that she would reveal all and to someone like Horace." He tipped the glass and drank the lot. "I'm going to hang for this."

"$\mathcal{M}$y main concern," Evie said as they were about to enter her house, "is that Martin will hang for a crime he didn't commit and the killer will get away with murder. By the time Martin finishes that bottle of whisky he will have convinced himself of his guilt."

"Are you going to tell the others about his affair?" Tom asked.

"Not unless I absolutely have to. It's not as if we have all the details." Evie checked the time. "I'm going up. I suppose you'll be headed straight to the kitchen. I'll see you later for drinks."

When she reached the top of the stairs, Evie laughed. Edgar had cornered Tom and was subjecting him to a thorough line of questioning about Clara Ashwood's well-being. She walked into her room shaking her head and smiling.

"Oh, milady. I was just laying out your dress for this evening," Millicent said.

"Millicent! You came up."

"Well, I was hardly going to leave poor Edgar all alone in London what with his infatuation with Miss Clara Ashwood."

"Yes, I know you came up to London, I meant… up here."

"Oh, yes. Caro is currently busy being Lady Carolina Thwaites. I hope you don't think I'm being too forward, milady, but you are indulging her. It might all go to her head."

Where had she heard that before? Evie laughed. She removed her hat and glanced at the door. She expected Toodles to burst in at any moment with demands for more information. "Is that the general consensus below stairs?"

"Not at all, milady. I've never heard a bad word said about you, and I doubt anyone would ever dare to speak a word against you. They've become accustomed to you blurring the lines and making up your own rules."

Evie had no idea how to respond to that. Lines of distinction existed because they made everyone's life less complicated…

"Caro gave me strict instructions, milady. Tonight, you are to wear the copper dress with the black lace trim."

Evie grinned. "We don't want to get on Caro's bad side, so we should do as we are told but as you already know, I do favor more cheerful colors."

"Yes, Caro warned me you might put up some resistance and she said to remind you—"

"Yes, yes. I have been presented." Glancing at the door again, she asked, "Has my granny asked about me?"

"No, milady. They all returned a half hour ago and

have been busy in the library. Caro… or rather, Lady Carolina Thwaites is with them. She wishes to know if you would like her to join you for dinner."

"Yes, otherwise I'll have to repeat every single conversation."

Millicent's eyebrow hitched up.

"I suppose you disapprove."

"It's not my place to say so, milady."

"Anything else?"

"I believe I heard Lady Woodridge say she needed to use the telephone."

"Which Lady Woodridge?"

"Lady Sara, milady. She said she had plenty of connections and someone ought to know something."

They spent the next half hour chatting about a proposed trip to the museum and plans for one of the servant's upcoming birthday.

A light knock at the door preceded Tom's entrance. "Are you decent?"

"Always. Come in." Glancing at him, Evie added, "Toodles will approve of your dinner jacket but I'm sure Henrietta will roll her eyes and mistake you for a waiter. You know she doesn't think much of tuxedos."

"Henrietta has acquired a degree of tolerance. I doubt she'll even notice." Tom leaned against the window. "I tried going into the library but Edgar warned me to stay away. What do you think that's about?"

"Your guess is as good as mine. I doubt Toodles has half the information we do. I'd say they're working on a jigsaw puzzle, trying to put together the little they have and fill in the gaps with whatever they can come up with."

"If I didn't know better, I'd say she has brought out

the competitive spirit in you." Tom picked up a scent bottle, smelled it, and set it down. He worked his way through the rest of the perfume flasks. To her surprise, he handed her one. "Dark and mysterious with a hint of the orient."

Evie excused herself to go into the next room to change. "You can keep talking. I'll hear you. By the way, have you recovered your strength?"

"Not entirely. Cook wouldn't let me spoil my dinner. She gave me a small chunk of bread and cheese to keep me going."

"Oh, I just remembered something else I meant to ask you. When we visited Wilfred, I noticed you cast your eyes over his desk. Did you happen to see anything of interest?"

"Indeed, I did. Loulou's first draft. It was written across the front page."

"She must have been busy writing it at Halton House. I wonder if she'll let people know."

"Do you want her to? It's bound to give everyone ideas. Soon you'll have people peering through your windows waiting to see you in action."

"I believe I have already gained a reputation for meddling. Nothing she says will be news to anyone." Evie emerged from her boudoir and went to stand in front of a mirror. "I've been thinking about the whisky. The detective could at least find out if any of the Halton House guests made recent purchases."

"It could just as easily have come from someone's cellar," Tom murmured.

"I can't picture Clara Ashwood with a cellar but the others might be at risk of becoming suspects. What sort of whisky would have you salivating and eager to taste it? I think I've already asked you that…"

Tom crossed his arms and looked up at the ceiling. "Macallan. Glenfiddich… They're considered to be supreme whiskies."

"Is there a particular vintage we should look at?"

Tom chuckled. "No. Unlike wine, whisky doesn't age or improve in a bottle. I believe it's all about the cask. I might be wrong."

"As you can see, I'm not much of a whisky drinker."

"Hold still, milady." Millicent adjusted a headband and warned, "This is the way Caro told me you should wear it."

"Millicent, you have done a wonderful job. In case I forget, please remind me to invite Lady Manners to tea." Turning to Tom, she added, "I need to find out if I'm about to star in another story."

When they made their way downstairs, they stopped half way to listen to the voices wafting from the drawing room.

"They sound excited," Tom said. "Do you have a plan?"

Evie grinned. "I'm tempted to pretend we did as I suggested this morning and ended up having lunch and nothing else."

"Yes, well… You're on your own. I couldn't even pretend to have spent the day enjoying a good meal."

Stepping inside the drawing room, she exclaimed, "Ah, the detective is here."

Toodles sat next to him. "Either someone broke into his house and contaminated a bottle of whisky or the killer gave him a bottle and if you ask me, it would have been something extraordinarily good."

The detective nodded. "Yes, very insightful."

"What about motives, detective. Have you come up with anything interesting?" Toodles asked.

Henrietta looked up. "Here's Evangeline. You were quite right this morning. We had tremendous fun. Thank you for suggesting it."

Still surprised by her granny's astute remark which sounded so similar to her own, Evie accepted a cocktail from Edgar and sat next to Henrietta. "And what did you ladies get up to?"

"We made your chauffeur earn his keep. He drove us all around London."

"Chasing after you, Birdie," Toodles said.

Evie tried to look surprised but ended up laughing. "We noticed."

"I see." Henrietta shared a knowing look with the others. "You gave us the slip. I told Toodles you had been at the theater. I could still pick up the scent of your perfume."

"Really?"

"Jasmine. Remember, I gave you that fragrance," Henrietta explained. "But Phillipa insisted she hadn't seen you all day. Lady Carolina suggested you might have preempted our intentions to follow you and so engaged Phillipa's help in misleading us. However, we were lucky to have her expertise and she then suggested you might have been paying visits to everyone who attended the house party."

"Cousin Carolina is very astute," Evie murmured and turned to the detective to look for signs of the letters he had promised to show her. Had he remembered to bring them?

Interpreting her curiosity, the detective gave his dinner jacket pocket a pat and gave her a small nod.

Evie nearly jumped out of her seat. He *had* brought the letters. Glancing at Tom, she saw him smile.

She was so tempted to suggest they forego dinner in favor of reading the letters but Tom would never forgive her.

Toodles cleared her throat. "Are you going to make us ask about your day? Fine, I'll ask. Did you discover anything useful and will you share it with us?"

"I will share," Evie agreed, "but I require absolute discretion." She told them about Martin Gate's affair. "It seems Horace Gibbins enjoyed wielding control over people. We have collected a few accounts, including one from Lady Stafford who said he had threatened to discredit her. Oh, wait. We actually heard that from Loulou."

"Lady Manners knew about it?" Henrietta sounded shocked.

Evie nodded.

The detective finished his drink and set his glass down. "You don't believe Martin Gate or Lady Stafford felt inclined to commit murder?"

"No, I don't. Martin Gate is too honorable. He agreed to pick up Horace's tab at the restaurant in order to safeguard his lover's identity. The amount would have been insignificant to him. As for Helen…" Evie shrugged. "I believe Helen is more interested in carving out a new life for herself."

"Everyone has their limits, Lady Woodridge. From what I understand, Lady Stafford made a public display of her feelings toward Clara Ashwood at your house party by tipping a glass of wine on the actress. Until then, she had reserved her opinions."

True.

Evie wished Edgar would hurry up and announce dinner. She needed to read those letters. There had to be something there to explain Lauren Wilkes' relationship with Horace Gibbins. Hopefully, something incriminating.

Taking a quiet sip of her drink, Evie realized she had been putting a great deal of effort to clear her friends of any wrongdoing.

Then again, she didn't consider Clara Ashwood a friend. And yet, she had given the thespian equal time.

Finally, Edgar received the signal from a footman and announced, "Dinner is served."

Tom shot to his feet and straightened his jacket.

Evie couldn't resist the temptation. She took hold of his arm and tugged him back.

His look of utter disbelief had her bursting into laughter which she struggled to contain. Leaning in, she whispered, "I merely wished to tell you the detective has brought the letters."

"Don't, whatever you do, ask me to forego dinner. Anything but that, Countess."

"I wouldn't dream of it. However…"

"I don't like the sound of that." He looked at the others who were all waiting for Evie to precede them into the dining room. "You're holding up the line. Walk and talk, Countess. Walk and talk." He grabbed hold of her hand and, this time, he did the tugging.

CHAPTER 17

"*T*here we were, our heads poking out of the motor car windows trying to catch sight of the roadster but Evie and Tom gave us the slip..."

Chasing a pea around her plate, Evie listened to Caro, or rather, Cousin Carolina, sharing the adventures they'd enjoyed that day.

Caro continued, "Mr. Martin Gate had already experienced one round with the detective and then, there we were, assailing him with a barrage of questions. The poor man looked dizzy."

"Yes," Toodles agreed. "But we only succeeded in wearing him out for Birdie. He spilled all the beans to her."

The detective laughed. "Perhaps I should employ that tactic in future. Send Lady Woodridge in first to question suspects and wear them out for me."

Evie failed to see the humor in the detective's remark even as everyone else found it amusing.

Since sitting down, Tom hadn't shifted his attention

away from his meal. Waiting for him to finish the last course, Evie watched him close his eyes. She imagined him trying to commit the meal to memory.

"I told you there'd be a nice spread for dinner." Although, admittedly, the servings were always quite small. Evie leaned toward him and whispered, "Would you like another helping of roast?"

"I'd prefer to leave room for dessert." He grinned. "It's a summer pudding."

Heavens. One more course.

For some annoying reason, everyone appeared to be taking their time with each course.

"Since it's only you and the detective, you might want to join us in the drawing room instead of remaining behind."

"And miss out on brandy and cigars?"

"But you don't smoke cigars or drink brandy."

"There's always a first time."

"Is this about me denying you a proper meal today?"

"No, it's about me not being able to move after the meal I've had." He smiled. "Fine. There might also be some backlash involved for nearly starving me."

"Well, could you be quick about it, please? I'd like to read those letters. I'm sure you do too."

"And I have no doubt the detective will oblige me by showing them to me… while we have our brandy and cigars."

"You wouldn't dare."

"Another sherry, Toodles?" Edgar offered.

"Why? I didn't have one the first time you offered." Toodles held up her empty whisky tumbler. "Fill me up, Edgar."

"Certainly... Toodles."

Evie's eyes bounced between the door and the clock on the fireplace. How long did it take to smoke a cigar? She had a good mind to barge in and throw a bucket of cold water on Tom.

"Cousin Evie." Caro crossed the drawing room and settled next to Evie.

"Cousin Carolina. Thank you for amusing us during dinner with your adventures."

"Your grandmother insisted I join them."

So it had been Toodles' idea to follow them.

Caro lowered her voice to a whisper, "I hope... I didn't abuse the privilege, milady."

It took a moment for Evie to decipher the remark. "I invited you to step into the role, Caro. And I'm glad you went along. I can always trust you to be my eyes and ears."

Caro looked away. "Well... my loyalties are divided at the moment."

"What do you mean?"

"Your grandmother is keeping a tally of all the information we gathered and she is matching it against yours. She wants to know who can figure out the identity of the killer first."

"My grandmother... is competing against me?"

"To put it bluntly, yes."

"And you are on her team?"

"Only by accident, milady. If I'd had the choice, I would have picked your side."

Henrietta cleared her throat as if to draw attention to

herself. "My dear Carolina. I hope you are not sharing our tactics."

"Oh, I wouldn't dream of it." Caro mouthed an apology and moved away from Evie.

"I seem to recall sharing information with you," Evie complained. "Why have I suddenly been cast adrift?"

Her granny wagged a finger at her. "You gave us the slip, missy."

"Strictly speaking, Tom is the one responsible for losing you. I had nothing to do with that. You would think we'd pull together our resources for the greater good. There is a killer out there. What if they strike again?"

They all looked down at the glasses they held.

"That's right." Evie nodded.

"What nonsense," Sara said. "Why would anyone want to poison us?"

"Because, without knowing it, you might have asked the right question and the killer thinks you are onto them," Evie argued.

Toodles brought out her notebook. "Birdie makes a valid point. We should work together. You go first."

"Shouldn't we wait for Tom and the detective to join us?" Sara asked.

"I don't see why we should." Henrietta took a sip of her sherry. "They might be discussing the case as we speak."

"Well? Are you going to share what you have?" Toodles asked.

Evie wanted to argue the point saying she had already shared information. To her relief, Tom and the detective made their entrance. Evie couldn't help frowning. When did cigars and brandy become more important than finding a killer?

Evie stretched out her hand. She could not have looked more demanding.

"My lady, I hope you realize I am breaking all my rules."

"Yes, yes. Now hand them over, please." The tidy bundle consisted of nearly fifty letters. Horace and Lauren Wilkes had corresponded over the course of several months. Nearly a year, Evie thought.

"They are all in order of dates received. Those are the letters sent by Miss Lauren Wilkes," the detective explained.

Evie skimmed through the first one. Lauren's penmanship left a lot to be desired. She began well enough, but as the letter progressed, the writing slanted in all directions.

She read through several of them before Henrietta sniffed. "You could at least read them out loud."

"She describes the weather, Henrietta. As well as all the people she met at parties. She mentions living in Sunset Boulevard and meeting someone named Rudolph Valentino."

"Oh, he's an up and coming star," Toodles said. "I saw him in *Delicious Little Devil* last year. There's a rumor that one of the characters is based on someone who had an affair with the King of Portugal."

"Lauren Wilkes appears to be asking for advice," Evie said and rushed through the next letter. "Oh, yes. Here she mentions wanting to return to England and she asks Horace if he has any suggestions about where she should live." She picked up the next letter. "In this one, Lauren thanked Horace for the advice."

After reading a dozen letters Evie sat back. "She sought his guidance in everything, including what to wear. Why would she do that? She doesn't strike me as the type to rely on anyone."

Toodles smiled. "Some women do that."

"What?"

"Defer. They yield all responsibilities and decisions to someone else. Usually a man. But I've seen some do it with their mothers-in-law."

Sara looked at Evie. "Did you do that with me?"

"Well… not exactly." However, she had made a point of taking the road of least resistance and maintaining the status quo at Halton House even though she'd known other women would have tried to put their personal mark on the house.

So… Lauren had tried to insinuate her way into his life to the point of becoming dependent on him.

She finished reading the letters, skimming through most of them and reading some parts out loud.

"I think she tried to make him feel special," Caro said. "Indispensable."

"That's a fine observation, Cousin Carolina," Evie said. "She would have known Horace Gibbins could help her gain entry into the theater world. Someone in his position would have jumped at the chance to claim credit for a thespian's success."

"Does that mean she's off the hook?" Henrietta asked. "Surely, if she needed Horace Gibbins… then she wouldn't kill him."

Evie brushed her finger across her chin. "Clara Ashwood complained about Horace taking over. What if, once Lauren arrived, she realized she had given him too much control over her life? She might have wanted to get rid of him. Especially if she realized she no longer needed him to get a role."

"But why kill him?" Sara asked.

"Because if she went about it on her own, he would feel snubbed. This was a man who could make or break a career. And, let's not forget, she had the opportunity to bring wood alcohol with her from America."

"Detective? Will you act on that suspicion?" Toodles asked.

"I believe I will, Toodles."

Evie nibbled the edge of her lip. "Yes, the more I think about it, the more convinced I am she had something to do with it. Martin Gate told us Horace enjoyed wielding his power. He'd also been interfering with Phillipa's directing. No doubt, he thought he could get away with it because he knew Phillipa would have been afraid of receiving a bad review for her play. He could have sung Clara Ashwood's praises while destroying the play."

Toodles shifted to the edge of her chair. "Are you now saying Phillipa had a reason for killing Horace?"

"Heavens. No."

"What about Wilfred Hartigan and Lady Manners?" Sara asked. "Are they in the clear?"

The detective cleared his throat.

Evie looked up at him. "Detective?"

"As a matter of fact…" He raked his fingers through his hair. "Lady Manners is in the process of writing a mystery."

"Oh, yes," Evie said. "She mentioned it today and Tom saw the first draft on Wilfred's desk."

"One of the characters in the story is based on Horace

Gibbins," the detective said. "Somehow, he found out about it and threatened Lady Manners with a libel suit."

Why hadn't Loulou confided in her?

Toodles clucked her tongue. "He could dish it out but he couldn't take it."

"How did he find out?" Evie asked.

The detective looked down at his shoes. "Lady Manners believes her maid might have read through the manuscript and shared the information with the other maids at Halton House and that's how it all got back to Horace Gibbins."

Evie glanced at Caro who looked mystified. Clearly, the information hadn't reached her.

In any case, Evie insisted she couldn't see Loulou as a killer. She didn't have it in her, but she could hardly use that excuse to defend her friend.

She shook her head. "No, it can't be Lady Manners."

"It can't be easy being a widow," the detective observed. "She needs to make her way in the world..."

"No, she doesn't have any financial concerns. The estate was settled in her favor."

When Edgar set a tray of coffee down on a table, Caro jumped to her feet and helped herself to a cup. "What about Wilfred Hartigan?" she asked. "If Mr. Horace Gibbins had given Lady Manners's book a bad review or sued her, it would have reflected badly on Wilfred Hartigan's publishing house."

True.

"Oh, but he's such a jolly nice fellow," Toodles declared. "Surely he doesn't have it in him to kill someone. Besides, he suffered enough..."

"Granny!"

"Well, you must admit, you made the poor man your target."

"Unintentionally." Instead of waiting for Edgar to serve her a cup of coffee, Evie surged to her feet and walked across the room to stretch her legs and distract herself. "Since we know the cause of death, it is now imperative to find out who had the means to obtain the wood alcohol," she reasoned and turned toward the detective.

"It seems everyone who attended your house party had some sort of motive," he said.

"Phillipa is the exception. She did not come to Halton House. Besides, she would never be so foolish." Evie took a sip of her coffee and set the cup down. "Horace had already been stumbling around when he left Halton House." She strolled around the drawing room and came to a stop. "Someone might have added the wood alcohol to his flask or the bottle… No, that can't be right. He was traveling."

The detective nodded. "My apologies. I should have shared some pertinent information. Mr. Gibbins traveled with a small trunk specially designed for his whisky bottles."

Evie couldn't help laughing. "He traveled around with his own bar? That is taking his passion for drinking to extremes." She turned to Edgar. "Are all the bottles of whisky at Halton House accounted for?"

He raised an eyebrow. "Of course, my lady. I would have noticed something missing straightaway."

They all turned to the detective.

"At this point, we are widening the net and looking at people he liaised with before the house party."

Toodles shook her head. "I'm sorry, Birdie, but something tells me it's one of your friends. Someone went to the trouble of poisoning him slowly. They would have taken great delight in watching his decline."

"If that's the case, Granny, we have to narrow down the suspects to everyone present at the theater. The killer would have made sure to be around him, waiting for the moment when he finally expired."

CHAPTER 18

$\mathcal{T}$he next morning, Evie went straight down to the library where she placed a telephone call to the housekeeper at Halton House. After their brief conversation, she telephoned the detective and passed on the information. Then she sat back and tried to decide what it all meant.

According to the housekeeper, a maid had indeed found mud tracks. At the time, she hadn't mentioned it because she hadn't seen the need for it. Evie decided this had to be a different maid to the one who'd complained about clothes being strewn on the floor...

Hearing the door open, she turned.

"There you are, Countess. Are we setting off some-where today? I wanted to know if I should ask the cook to prepare a picnic hamper to take with us."

Evie laughed. "You don't wish to take any risks."

He perched on the armrest of the sofa opposite her. "From now on, I intend being the perfect boy scout.

Always prepared." He gestured to the notebook on the small desk. "What have you been working on?"

Evie told him about her conversation with the housekeeper. "Not only did the maid find muddy tracks in one of the rooms, she cleaned out the chimney and found an old pair of work boots stashed inside it." Evie leaned forward. "She found them in the room Lauren Wilkes stayed in."

"She's your rose killer."

"It would appear so."

"You're still not convinced?"

"On the surface, it makes sense." She waved her hand. "Remember, we talked about Lauren possibly being jealous of Clara Ashwood. I'm actually relieved Lady Stafford had nothing to do with it." Evie set aside her notebook and got up. "It's strange. Despite Lauren Wilkes attacking the roses, I don't actually feel she tampered with Horace's whisky. It's just a feeling."

"Do you have any new suspicions?"

"I haven't had my breakfast yet." Evie chortled and brushed her hand across her face. "Heavens, I just remembered Henrietta saying someone should do something about Horace Gibbins. I'm glad no one else heard her. Otherwise, she would need to be added to the list. She might actually enjoy that."

"How did the detective react to the news about the boots?" Tom asked.

"It's solid proof... However, I can't help wondering what it proves."

"Are you thinking the boots might have been placed in Lauren's room by the killer?"

Evie sat up. "Oh... I hadn't thought of that. It's almost

an unrelated incident. Or is it?" Evie gave it some thought and then got up. "We have a long day ahead of us. It's opening night and I'd like to drop by the theater this afternoon to see if Phillipa needs anything."

The dowagers and Toodles were already enjoying their breakfast.

"Ah, Birdie. We've been discussing what we'll be wearing for the opening night. Are we in mourning for Horace Gibbins?"

Henrietta shivered. "It will be a bleak affair with everyone wearing black."

"Must we?" Evie didn't want to mention the green and orange dress she had ordered from Mrs. Green.

"I suppose we should play it safe." Toodles accepted another cup of coffee from Edgar. "I envy the gentlemen who don't need to worry about this."

Sara buttered her toast as she said, "Did someone say Martin Gate had been in need of a story? I have spent the night tossing and turning, thinking about it."

"I believe Evangeline might have mentioned it. In any case, Mr. Gate has his scoop. Oh, I suppose that should make him a prime suspect. The fact he revealed the so-called secret Horace used to blackmail him with shouldn't mean he is innocent. He might have sacrificed that information in order to make himself appear to be a victim."

"Henrietta, that is marvelous reasoning," Toodles offered.

Smiling, the dowager inclined her head. "I believe I am beginning to enjoy this business of investigating a crime. Evangeline, this could become a family affair."

"Oh, I can't wait to tell the detective. He will be so pleased," Evie teased.

Henrietta added, "When Evangeline sets herself up in her detecting agency, we could act as consultants."

"Will you expect a fee?" Evie asked.

"Oh, no. My dear, Evangeline. I have not worked a day in my life. I do not mean to start now."

"Not worked?" Toodles sounded surprised. "I thought country ladies kept themselves busy and thrived on spreading good cheer among their neighbors and those less fortunate. Every time Birdie writes to me, she tells me about someone or other falling ill and everyone making sure they are well looked after. Then there are the fetes held to collect money for one worthy cause or another and the garden parties."

"Oh, we do what we can, but I have never thought of any of that as work. Do you, Sara?"

"No, not at all. As you said, one simply does what one can." Sara gave Evie a small smile. "I must say, I agree with Henrietta. We could be quite helpful... in our limited capacity."

"Oh, don't sell yourself short," Toodles chided.

Henrietta leaned in and murmured, "I believe Sara was trying to be modest."

"Are we all wearing black tonight?" Sara asked. "Has it been decided?"

Evie nodded. "I might not have a choice because Caro believes the Countess of Woodridge should always dress the part."

Henrietta gasped. "I've just had the most unnerving thought. What if Mr. Gibbins makes an appearance tonight?"

"As a ghost?" Toodles asked.

"Yes. I would hate to be the person sitting where he

died. Oh, that reminds me of something I read in an issue of Country Life. It was a letter from someone curious to know if dogs see ghosts. He wrote to say a retriever of high pedigree and even higher intelligence enjoyed the comforts of a favorite armchair in the smoking-room. She always enjoyed sleeping there quietly, when suddenly, one day, she woke in great distress and alarm. Jumping from the chair, she rushed about in great excitement. Then she shot out of the room. She never entered the smoking-room again. When the owner tried to coax her inside, she would show signs of anxiety and terror, whimpering and howling."

"Heavens," Sara exclaimed. "Perhaps someone should have a word with Phillipa and suggest she keep Horace's chair empty… as a sign of respect, of course. We wouldn't want Phillipa obsessing about a ghost."

Evie laughed. "On the contrary. Phillipa would welcome news about a ghost."

"She should look on the bright side," Toodles suggested. "We watched only a portion of the play and thought it quite amusing. The audience will be distracted by that, at least."

"I wonder who will take over from Horace Gibbins?" Sara asked. "Someone will have to review the play."

"I doubt anyone has given that any thought." Evie watched Tom get up and help himself to another plate full of bacon and eggs, which earned him a raised eyebrow look from Edgar.

Tom happened to notice it. "The Countess is a hard taskmaster."

"Heavens. Anyone who heard you would think I make you run alongside the motor car."

He smiled. "It hasn't come to that yet."

"Evangeline, have you made any sense of the contradictory information you received from Lauren Wilkes and Clara Ashwood?"

"I suspect Lauren Wilkes wished to protect her pride. I doubt she'd feel comfortable having people think she is only good enough to be an understudy."

"Do be careful when you go out today, Birdie. Try to avoid accepting drinks from anyone you know."

"As opposed to people I don't know?"

Her granny shrugged. "Why would a complete stranger want to kill you?"

Evie set her cup down. "Edgar."

"Yes, my lady."

"Have you given everyone instructions to be wary of unexpected gifts?" Seeing his puzzled expression change to concern, Evie smiled. "Not to worry. Please make sure everyone is well informed. I should have mentioned it earlier."

Toodles laughed. "Next you'll be employing food tasters."

Tom looked up. "I suppose that task would fall on me. I might need to draw lines."

"I guess you didn't notice I haven't touched my eggs," Evie said. "I've been waiting to see what effect they have on you." Evie looked down at her plate. They had spoken about it a couple of times so she couldn't claim to be entirely oblivious of the possibility. While reason told her there wouldn't be anyone interested in killing her or her guests, one simply couldn't tell. The mind of a killer remained a foreign place to Evie. "Edgar, I trust you have taken care of the drinks for tonight's event."

"Yes, my lady. We brought several cases of champagne from Halton House. I'm happy to report there were no breakages. We will be transporting the bottles and glasses to the theater later in the afternoon."

"Thank you. I knew I could trust you to make all the arrangements."

"It's comforting to hear you getting on with it, Evangeline. I suppose this means you have decided to leave the matter in the detective's capable hands or are we now going to see you in action, rushing around to solve the murder before the curtain goes up?"

"The only way I am going to find the killer is if he or she walks right up to me and confesses. Now, if you'll excuse us, Tom and I are going to visit Phillipa to make sure she has the moral support she needs."

Tom looked up from his half-eaten breakfast. "Now? As in… right now? I thought you said we were going in the afternoon. As in… after lunch."

Evie rolled her eyes. "Whenever you're ready."

A horde of unexpected visitors delayed Evie's trip to the theater. Somehow, everyone had found out Horace Gibbins had stayed with her. Those who hadn't known about Phillipa's play were now intent on attending.

"We might have to put Phillipa on the suspect list, after all," Tom mused.

"Oh, my goodness. Not even in jest." Regardless, Evie couldn't help laughing.

As they drove up to the theater, it came as no surprise

to see a sign across the billboard saying the play had been booked out.

Tom and Evie stared at in.

Tom tipped his hat back. "One has to wonder… Who stands to benefit from a sold-out play?"

"In the long run? Willie. I'm sure he'll inherit his father's fortune. Are you prepared to question him?" Evie asked.

Tom looked toward his roadster and at Willie. "I wouldn't put it past him."

Hurrying inside, Evie made her way to the front row where she found Phillipa going through the script. "How is the star of the show today?"

"She had a little fainting spell," Phillipa said, her eyes filled with concern. "We were inspecting the stage, making sure everything was where it had to be when she swooned." Phillipa lowered her voice. "If I didn't know better, I'd say Clara is putting on an act."

"I never asked this… how long has she been suffering from this malaise?"

"Let me think." Phillipa looked up at the stage and tapped a pen against her lip. "We were at a restaurant when she excused herself saying she felt ill. We'd met to discuss the role so that must have been a couple of months ago. Everything happened so quickly. One moment I was thinking about writing a play, then I had a script and I met Horace Gibbins who introduced me to Clara Ashwood and… here we are. He even organized the theater for me. And that was a miracle since places are booked from year to year. I know it's not the best theater but it's in the theater district. Horace knew how to pull strings and get what he wanted."

Had that cost him his life? He might have secured the theater through foul means. More blackmail! "Do you know if the detective spoke with the owner of the theater?"

Phillipa nodded. "He's a sweet man. He's actually a lawyer. He inherited the theater from his father and keeps it going for his son Willie."

Evie knew if the detective had found a lead, he would have shared it with her. At least, she hoped so.

"What about Horace. Did he show signs of illness back then?"

"I can't say that I noticed. Are you thinking Horace knew the killer for a long time?" Phillipa's voice sounded flat.

"Clara Ashwood said he left a trail of enemies behind him. It's possible the killer might have been plotting Horace's demise for some time."

Phillipa's shoulders slumped. She checked her watch and pushed out a big breath. "Three hours and counting. What can possibly go wrong?"

"Absolutely nothing. Your play has sold out." Evie gave her a bright smile. "How are you? Are you excited? It's opening night."

Phillipa managed a smile, but it didn't last. "I have tried my best and despite Clara's health issues, her performances during rehearsals have been wonderful."

"The little I've seen I thoroughly enjoyed," Evie offered. "Edgar tells me everything will be in place for the after-show celebrations. He should be along soon. I heard him mention something about setting up trolleys to wheel onto the stage once the audience clears out." Evie looked up at the scenery. "I'd wanted to surprise you but I couldn't think of a way to pull it off other than to blind-fold you for the day and that wouldn't do at all." She looked over her shoulder for signs of Tom and saw Loulou making her way to the front row.

Phillipa jumped to her feet. "I forgot to mention. Lady Manners wants to interview me. She's doing a piece on the play. Actually, she's reviewing it."

"She is?" Evie's heart jumped to her throat. Loulou hadn't mentioned it.

After an exchange of greetings, Evie said, "Keeping secrets, Loulou?"

Lady Manners threw her head back and laughed. "You know me, Evie. Always up to something but never saying anything about it."

"You seem to be throwing yourself into writing."

"Things are just falling on my lap. Martin Gate happened to mention wanting to write something about the play and since I'm working on a story which seems to be going nowhere, I decided to share my impressions of Phillipa's play."

"Lucky Martin." The newspaper owner had secured the scoop he'd needed and he now had someone writing a review.

Evie left the two women to get on with the interview. Outside, she found Tom tossing a coin as he talked with Master Willie.

Seeing her, he handed over some money and went to open the passenger door for Evie. "I take it everything is going according to plan for Phillipa."

"I hope so. Let's head back to the house for afternoon tea."

Tom grinned. "You mean it?"

"Why so surprised?"

"This is the first time you've become so involved in a case you've ended up skipping meals."

"It's different this time. I happen to know everyone involved and Phillipa's livelihood is at stake."

CHAPTER 19

*T*hey returned to the house only to find it full of more uninvited guests eager to see if they could secure tickets to the performance.

"Well, if I didn't have a reputation for courting murder before, I do now," Evie murmured.

Toodles sidled up to Evie and said, "The dowagers and I were just about to set off after you when Edgar announced another visitor. Then, they just kept coming. What did we miss?"

"Nothing." And that worried Evie. If the detective didn't find the culprit soon, he might have to close the case.

To Evie's surprise, no sooner did one guest leave than another one arrived.

Evie spent the next hour listening to Toodles entertaining the guests by giving various versions of the event she had witnessed at the theater. In one of them, she declared Horace Gibbins had flung his arms out before toppling over.

When the last guest finally left, Evie confided in Tom, "If I didn't know better, I'd say they all expect something to happen tonight."

Clearing his throat, Edgar excused himself, "We will be heading off to the theater with the champagne now, my lady."

"Heavens, there's been a whirlwind of activity, Evangeline. I'm not sure if I will be happy to return to Halton House or if I'll miss all this excitement, not to mention the anticipation. Did anything happen at the theater? With so many people coming and going I haven't had the opportunity to ask."

Evie decided to keep the news about Lady Manners being engaged to write a review to herself. She had simply known her too long to believe her capable of cold-blooded murder.

If only they could get through the night without any mishaps…

"Miss Phillipa must be excited," Caro said.

"She's working toward it." Evie set the soap aside and focused on clearing her mind but her thoughts had other ideas.

There is no such thing as a perfect crime.

Why hadn't Lauren Wilkes returned the work boots to wherever she'd found them? Why stash them in the fireplace where someone would eventually find them?

"Someone set her up."

She pictured Lady Stafford reaching the end of her tether. She'd been forced to make polite conversation with her husband's lover and she decided to take action by hacking the roses and then clearing herself of any suspicion by hiding the boots in someone else's room.

The scene unfolded in her mind as clear as daylight.

Evie closed her eyes and lowered herself until the bath water covered her mouth.

"If you stay in there much longer, you'll turn into a prune, milady."

Evie dried herself and turned her attention to dressing for that night's event.

She slipped into her dress, her back teeth gritting, but she refused to say anything. Fuming, she watched Caro making the necessary adjustments. When she finished, Evie looked at her reflection and pushed the words out, "What happened to the green and orange dress I wanted?"

Caro swung away and busied herself tidying Evie's clothes. "Everyone is so excited. They've been talking of nothing else. Millicent has been fixing everyone's hair. They all want to look their best for the opening night."

"Caro!"

"Yes, milady?"

"Oh, never mind. I suppose you didn't even bother to speak with Mrs. Green about the dress."

"As a matter of fact, yes, I did. And she happened to agree with me. Black is more fitting for this occasion." She opened the jewelry case. "Your necklace will look splendid with that gown."

"Of course. You're right, but I feel I should at least put up some token resistance. Otherwise, what good is being the head of the house?" She looked over her shoulder at the clock. "I should get going. I promised Phillipa I'd arrive early to give her moral support."

"That's too kind of you, milady. Although, if you ask me, I think you should be making a grand entrance."

"It's Phillipa's special day, Caro. I think we'll forego the tiara."

Caro handed her a pair of earrings and as Evie put them on, Caro brought out the tiara.

Evie groaned. "Caro!"

"But the outfit is not complete without it, milady."

"Well, it will just have to be."

"What will people think?"

"Caro. Do I look as if care what people think?"

Caro's bottom lip stuck out. "I thought you cared what I thought."

"I do and I thank you for being so attentive. Now, I'm sure you have to sort out your own clothes. I'll see you later tonight."

Evie hurried out of her room and met Tom at the top of the stairs.

"Countess, you look magnificent. Any news from the detective?"

Evie laughed. "No, I haven't heard any news. I'm sure the detective is just hoping we all forget about the case and get on with things. I only hope he does not make a dramatic entrance at the theater and arrest someone in the middle of the third act."

"Does that mean you didn't contact him?"

"Why would I?"

"To tell him about Lady Manners writing the review for the play. I thought we decided that made her a suspect."

"I said no such thing." Evie hurried down the stairs.

"But you expressed concern."

"Only because I felt she might need to explain herself."

"It does give her motive," Tom murmured.

"Loulou doesn't need the reviewer's job. She only took it because it happened to come along. It's definitely not something she would kill for. And, by the way, you look splendid."

Tom adjusted his black tie. "Thank you."

"Oh, my. Look at you both," Henrietta exclaimed. She stood at the bottom of the stairs looking up at them. "The detective telephoned to say he'd like to meet you at the theater. Although, he might be held up. Toodles took the telephone from me insisting she needed to speak with him."

When they reached the bottom of the stairs, Evie headed toward the front door while Tom hesitated.

"Tom?"

"Do you mean to tell me we are leaving now? Right now?" he asked. "I heard someone mention a light supper before the theater."

Henrietta nodded. "Oh, yes. We can't possibly go to the theater on an empty stomach."

Evie tugged Tom along. "You can have a late dinner."

Edgar stood by the door and held out the theater tickets.

"Thank you, Edgar. Please make sure everyone gets off all right. Phillipa needs all the support we can give her."

"Evangeline," Henrietta called out. "You've forgotten your tiara."

Evie waved. As she strode out of the house she thought she heard the dowager murmuring something about needing to uphold standards.

Catching Tom's raised eyebrow, Evie said, "It really would have been too much. Here, have a scotch mint."

Arriving at the theater, Evie spotted Willie. "I suppose you arranged for him to keep an eye on your roadster. Won't it be rather late for him?"

Before Tom could answer, a constable emerged from the theater, followed by the detective.

"I daresay, the roadster will be in good hands," he said. "I actually asked Willie to make sure there would be a space available for me right outside the theater. He charged me extra for the service. Little rascal. He's cleaning me out."

Willie greeted Evie and opened the passenger door for her.

"I am not paying for that," Tom warned.

Willie gave him a wide grin and revealed a front tooth missing.

"But he did such a splendid job, Tom. Surely he deserves recognition."

Tom tipped his hat. "You did a fine job, Master Willie."

Shaking her head, Evie walked toward the front entrance. "Detective. Please tell me you are not here to make an arrest."

"My lady, I wouldn't dream of ruining Miss Phillipa's night. If any arrests are to be made, I will wait until tomorrow."

Seeing the edge of his lips quirk up, Evie scooped in a breath. "You are jesting. Thank you. I needed that. I don't know about you, but I am feeling quite nervous. There's no such thing as a perfect crime but I fear the killer is about to prove us wrong." Evie told the detective about Lady Manners stepping into Horace Gibbins' shoes to review the play. "I couldn't help it. For a moment, I wondered if she might have a solid motive. But if we think about it, everyone appears to benefit from Horace's death. So, everyone has a possible motive."

The detective nodded in agreement. "Reliable forensic evidence has brought us this far. Rest assured, it will secure a conviction."

"How can you say that? You haven't found the bottle of whisky."

"Actually, we have." He tapped his nose. "Please keep the information to yourself."

"Was it a special bottle?"

"No, but we're hoping something will come up. Mr. Gibbins kept a list of all his whisky bottles, recording all details including his experiences drinking it. I have someone going through his journals to see if anything jumps out. I'm hoping there will be some sort of mention of a gift. But the man had been drinking for many years so my detective has his work cut out for him. He is being thorough and covering the last couple of months."

Evie crossed her fingers and hoped his findings led him to the killer. "I'm glad you are here, detective. Your presence is very reassuring."

"Are you really concerned something will happen to ruin opening night?"

"A part of me wants to believe the killer's confidence will work against him and he'll make a false move. I think he'll expect everyone to drop their guards." Evie was about to go in, when she stopped. "Detective, I meant to ask. Did Horace Gibbins have any family? I don't know why it didn't occur to ask until now. We have been fixating on anyone and everyone he came into contact with recently."

"We've spoken to some elderly relatives." The detective smiled.

"I'm sorry, I didn't mean to question your tactics."

"It's standard procedure, my lady. It's quite common practice for us to look at those closest to the victims. There have been cases of family members taking out insurance policies on someone and then helping them along…"

Tom approached them. "The street is swarming with police officers. If the killer shows up and puts a foot wrong, they'll pounce on him."

Evie looked up and down the street. She saw several men dressed smartly for the evening. "In disguise?"

"Yes."

"Did Edgar happen to include food in his delivery today?" Tom asked.

"I believe so."

Tom took Evie's arm and tugged her inside. "When were you going to tell me?"

Walking into the empty auditorium, Evie shivered. Stagehands were busy running around. The curtains closed and moments later, opened. By the time she and Tom made it to the front row, the curtains had been drawn again. A man walked past carrying a bouquet of red roses. When Evie asked where they might find Phillipa, the man pointed backstage.

They made their way there. When they came up to the first dressing room, they heard someone practicing their lines. Someone in the next dressing room was pacing. It seemed everyone had a different way of dealing with the buildup of excitement.

Evie shivered again. She could definitely feel some sort of energy in the air.

Phillipa rushed out of a room. Seeing them, she jumped. "So much to do. I had no idea it would be like this."

"Well, at least you're smiling."

"Sorry, I can't stop."

"I guess we don't need to worry about her," Evie said and peered inside Clara Ashwood's dressing room. The thespian emerged from behind a screen and stood in front of the mirror.

Evie drew in a deep breath before going in but she needn't have worried. She saw the roses but didn't pick up the strong scent.

"How are you feeling?"

Clara gave her a wide smile. "Couldn't be better. I live for opening nights."

"Break a leg," Evie said. She backed out of the room and guided Tom to the side of the stage. "Here we are. Nibble away." Looking up at him, she only then realized he'd been scanning their surroundings. She laughed. "You're not really expecting the killer to jump out and attack us."

"At this point, I have no idea what to expect."

CHAPTER 20

*T*he house lights dimmed. Someone had a fit of coughing. Evie heard people shuffling their feet and shifting. Others cleared their throats. Murmured conversations died down. A few seconds of silence later and the stage curtains opened to reveal a scene from a country house with a fireplace in the center, bookcases on either side, and a comfortable sofa with plump cushions.

A woman appeared dressed in a green and orange dress. Clara Ashwood came to a stop in the middle of the stage and swirled around on the spot.

"That's my dress!" Evie whispered.

Someone sitting behind her gasped. Evie didn't need to turn around to know it had been Caro.

With the performance on the way, she tried to lose herself in the story but her mind kept wandering.

This is a case of disguised murder...

Someone had gone to a lot of trouble to point fingers in several directions.

A wave of laughter swept around the auditorium

followed by appreciative clapping as the first act came to an end.

Whispered conversations swept around and then subsided as the audience settled down for the next act.

As the actors meandered their way along the next scene, the audience continued to respond with laughter and more clapping.

Everyone who had attended the house party sat in the row behind Evie. During the few lulls in the play, an over-whelming feeling of being watched swept over her and she spent the next scene trying to figure out who might be watching her. Before the curtain went up, she had managed to have a word with everyone so she knew who sat where.

Evie glanced behind her but didn't see anyone spearing their attention toward her.

Each and every one of her guests had gained some-thing from Horace Gibbins' death. But, in Evie's opinion, nothing significant enough to justify killing him.

A senseless, petty death with an equally senseless motive.

Martin Gate had said Horace had not needed money. Extorting those restaurant meals had been nothing but amusement to him. Now Martin was free to pursue his affair without consequences.

Lauren Wilkes had enjoyed a successful career in silent movies and now wished to make her mark on the stage. Evie assumed she'd needed Horace to help her achieve her dreams.

But did she?

What if she had come to see Horace as a hindrance?

Horace had been willing to help her... Or had he?

They'd only been able to get one side of the story from her letters to Horace. What if he had set conditions to helping her? Conditions which had seemed unpalatable to Lauren. Of everyone in the group, Lauren had the greatest opportunity to take action. She could have brought the wood alcohol with her from America.

However, the poison could be obtained right here in England.

As for Helen...

Lady Stafford, whose husband had been having an affair with Clara Ashwood...

Horace had threatened Lady Stafford. Had revenge driven her to kill him? Horace had planned on exposing Lady Stafford to divert attention away from Clara Ashwood. Such a public humiliation would have been too much for Helen...

Wilfred Hartigan planned on publishing Loulou's mystery. But Horace had threatened to sue Loulou for including him in her book. Also, she now had the job of reviewing the play.

Evie knew she couldn't allow years of friendship to stand in the way of finding the killer.

Out of all the possible motives, power stood out. Horace had wielded it with great relish and others had resented him for it.

Tom nudged her. That's when Evie realized the actors were taking their bow and the entire audience had erupted into applause and verbal accolades.

The killer had made a mistake.

"I'd love to watch the play again," Caro exclaimed. "Everyone loved it. To think, we're the first to see it and we know the scriptwriter. I must say, you were splendid, milady."

"Me?"

"That was you on the stage." Caro looked up at Tom. "And you. Miss Phillipa did a splendid job capturing your characters."

"Is that why everyone laughed so much?" Evie asked. "They were laughing at me?"

"And me, Countess. I guess that makes me your sidekick."

"Well... I'm not sure how I feel about that. Especially as I laughed right along with them." Evie turned to Caro. "And don't think I didn't notice Clara Ashwood wearing my dress."

Caro's cheeks reddened.

"Is there something I should know?"

"Well... Miss Phillipa telephoned earlier today. She needed some suggestions for the dress because Clara Ashwood had complained the one she had was all wrong."

"And you decided to be quite helpful."

"Milady, she was going to dress you in a horribly drab dress."

"Me?"

"As in you, the character on the stage."

"And so you decided to sacrifice the dress I wished to wear tonight..."

"All for the greater good, milady."

"That's called killing two birds with one stone. Helping Phillipa with an appropriate dress and forcing me to appear at the opening shrouded in black because it makes me look the part."

Caro expressed her dismay by saying, "Milady! There is still a killer at large. One would think you'd have better things to occupy yourself with."

Evie glanced at Tom. "Why are you grinning?"

"Because I'm amused by your maid telling you off."

While the audience made their way out of the auditorium, Evie and the rest of her guests made their way backstage. Meanwhile, Edgar and the stagehands set up the drinks and food on the stage in readiness for the cast members' appearance.

They all crowded around Phillipa to congratulate her. After Evie and Tom had their turn, they stepped aside and searched for the detective.

"My lady, you look preoccupied."

"That's because I am, detective." She looked over her shoulder and saw Lauren Wilkes staring at her with narrowed eyes and pursed lips.

Could she be wrong?

Evie scooped in a breath. "I think I know who the killer is."

At a signal from the detective, they made their way onto the stage where they settled by the fake fireplace.

The others began moving onto the stage too. Their chatter appeared to reach a crescendo and just when it seemed to quiet down, it rose again.

Evie didn't think it could get more exuberant until the star of the show appeared and everyone cheered and exclaimed their admiration for a fine performance.

Edgar jumped into action and hurried to pour the champagne and serve the drinks.

Glasses clinked. Conversations became more excited as the other cast members joined the group.

Evie accepted a glass of champagne and took a pensive sip.

The killer had made a mistake.

What did that mean?

Everyone who had come under suspicion had gone about their business as if nothing had happened. Although, Evie couldn't help thinking order had somehow been restored.

The detective cleared his throat and said, "I can't remember if I thanked your grandmother for her informed input. I must do so, just in case." He raised his glass to Evie. "Of course, I should also thank you for bringing Mr. Gibbins' death to my attention."

Evie smiled. "Toodles nearly overshadowed me." And she couldn't be happier. She'd worried so much about her granny disapproving of her antics, she hadn't once considered the possibility she might actually encourage her.

Evie searched the group for Lauren Wilkes. She found her talking with Henrietta.

Following her gaze, the detective observed, "The understudy looks happy enough. I wonder if she feels she missed her chance to shine. After all, Clara Ashwood had shown all signs of not being in the best condition."

"I'm sure the perfect role will come along for her," Evie murmured against her glass.

"Even without Mr. Gibbins' assistance?" Tom asked.

"She has solid credentials," Evie said.

"As a silent movie star," Tom mused. "The stage is a different kettle of fish."

"Lauren Wilkes impressed Phillipa with her performance. She must have tremendous talent."

"Well, my lady? You said you'd unmasked the killer."

Evie straightened. "Tell me detective, how would you feel if someone came along? Another detective with a solid record?"

"There's plenty of crime to go around, my lady."

"Yes, but… this new detective has the support of higher ups who are willing to pave the way for him. You might be overlooked for promotions."

The detective shifted slightly. "I won't lie to you. I've seen it happen."

Evie watched Clara Ashwood take a bow. Someone called for a speech which she gladly gave. "I'm so glad she was able to perform tonight without any problems. Do you know… it's almost miraculous. One day she's fainting and the next, she's fine. More than fine. She's perfect."

"Do you think she staged her illness to gain sympathy and attention?" Tom asked.

Evie tapped her finger on the glass. "Just as the performance ended, I had a stray thought. The killer made a mistake."

"I guess it's back to work for me." The detective set his glass down. "Are you about to upstage me, my lady?"

"Never on purpose, detective." Evie sensed an idea taking shape in her mind. However, without solid proof it would sound ludicrous.

"All right," the detective said. "Let's hear it."

CHAPTER 21

"I assume you interviewed everyone at the theater."

"Yes, of course..." He brushed a hand across his chin. "You're about to tell me I missed something obvious."

"If you did, I did too. Perhaps we shouldn't jump to conclusions without the support of forensic evidence." How could they get it without alerting anyone? Could she sneak away by herself? Evie immediately dismissed the thought. She'd never do anything so silly as to put herself in danger.

"And where do you suggest we find it, my lady?"

Evie's confidence dwindled for a moment. "Nothing ventured, nothing gained," she murmured. "In the perfume flask, detective."

Tom frowned. "The rose perfume in Clara Ashwood's dressing room?"

Evie nodded. "Do you remember how we found Clara slumped on her dressing room table? She had just sprayed perfume in the room. Personally, I found it too pungent."

"Yes, my coat still reeks of it," Tom said.

"Before the performance, Tom and I went to wish her well. The roses were there, but I did not smell the strong perfume. She had no need of it tonight. Test it, detective. You never know what you might find, but I suspect there will be traces of wood alcohol."

He moved without hesitation, making a discreet exit.

Surprised, Evie said, "Well… I thought I would have to argue the point and do a better job of convincing him…"

"The perfume. How? Why?" Tom asked.

"I have no idea. That's the detective's job. I can only hazard a guess. I wouldn't be surprised if the detective finds a bottle of whisky in her dressing room. Horace Gibbins spent a great deal of time in there."

"Yes, but… Why would she spray the room?"

"To make herself sick. I suppose she could have feigned it. Even if the detective finds the toxic substance in the flask, he'll need some sort of confession out of Clara Ashwood. After all, she can claim someone else has been trying to poison her. She could even point the finger at Lauren Wilkes. For all we know, she might have planted some sort of evidence as a precaution. I really wouldn't be surprised if Clara Ashwood is responsible for hacking the roses and leaving the old boots in Lauren Wilkes' room." Evie glanced around the stage and laughed. "I could just as easily be pointing the finger of suspicion at one of the others."

"But you're focusing on Clara Ashwood. Why do you think she went to all that trouble?"

Evie didn't hesitate. "Jealousy. Pure and simple. She'd been Horace Gibbins' star for a long time, and along comes someone else who wishes to compete for the spotlight. Remember how quickly she referred to Horace in the past tense? It's possible I'm reading too much into it…" Evie took a sip of her drink. Even if the detective found the flask, they would have to wait until the next day for the perfume to be tested. "Of course, I could be wrong."

"Oh, you will be right either way," Tom said. "If the perfume contains wood alcohol, she will become a suspect… Or a victim. If it doesn't have wood alcohol, she will be cleared of suspicion."

And if they found wood alcohol in the perfume, Evie feared the detective would have a difficult job of proving Clara had poisoned herself. "Now that I think about it, I wonder if inhaling that substance can affect you?" Sighing, Evie finished her champagne.

"More champagne, my lady?" Edgar offered.

"Yes, please."

"Mr. Winchester?"

"Oh, yes. Just keep it coming."

"How am I ever going to make it up to Phillipa?" she whispered. Looking up, her eyes clashed with Lauren Wilkes' who appeared to be looking at her with a hint of curiosity. The Hollywood star had been relying on Horace Gibbins. She'd had the support of an influential man. He would have turned her into a star.

What would have become of Clara Ashwood?

Could she be right? Could jealousy really drive a person to commit murder?

Evie searched for Clara and found her looking straight at her. The intensity of the thespian's stare had Evie shifting.

She knows.

Evie took a deep swallow. Something about her expression must have alerted Clara.

The thespian looked toward the dressing rooms, took a step and stopped as if uncertain…

"What's going on?" Tom whispered.

"She knows," Evie whispered back, her tone filled with urgency.

In the midst of it all, the detective appeared and held up a small flask. No one but Evie and Tom noticed him. But that was enough for Clara Ashwood.

She swung toward the detective.

In that split second, Evie saw a wild expression in her eyes.

Seeing the detective standing there, holding up the flask, Clara froze on the spot.

Tom and Evie shifted to the edge of the sofa.

"What now?" Evie asked.

"You don't leave my side… or sight. I mean it, Countess."

"Well, I'm hardly going to go for a stroll now… Am I?"

No one else had become aware of the events unfolding. Evie noticed Toodles surrounded by several people, holding court, laughing at something she'd said. Then she noticed Evie looking at her.

Evie saw her grandmother instantly turn and look around.

"What is it about my face? I seem to be an open book. Everyone is reading it and finding out my every thought."

Tom grabbed hold of her hand.

Evie knew he wanted to make sure she wouldn't move from his side and she understood the full meaning of his intention when Clara Ashwood lunged for the perfume flask.

"Of all the silly things to do," Evie said. "She's just given herself away."

"You almost sound disappointed," Tom murmured.

"Yes. She could have talked her way out of it."

The detective reacted by lifting the flask out of her reach. This enraged the thespian. She emitted a wild growl.

Then she whipped her arm out and swung around. Everyone jumped back.

"Stay away from me. Stay away." Clara retreated.

"I don't understand it," Evie whispered. "It would make sense if she were holding a knife or a glass, but she's controlling everyone with nothing but her commanding voice." Evie gasped. "Oh, heavens."

Clara Ashwood grabbed hold of Toodles and pulled her against her.

"She's using my granny as a shield," Evie shrieked.

Releasing her hand, Tom surged to his feet and growled, "Stay."

Evie had no idea how Tom communicated with the detective. They moved together toward their target. Whatever they planned on doing, Toodles beat them to it.

Just before Tom and the detective could take hold of Clara, Toodles flung her arm out. She must have seen Edgar standing nearby with a tray and a bottle of champagne. Toodles snatched the bottle and swung it at Clara hitting her on the side of the head.

The hard thump mingled with the thespian's scream and everyone's gasp of surprise.

Evie sprung up and rushed toward her granny. "Are you all right?"

"Absolutely. This is the most excitement I've had in years."

When Evie heard the thespian coming to, she turned toward her and growled, "Oh, I have a good mind to kick you. But... But I've been presented."

"I haven't." Caro rushed forward and gave the thespian a swift kick in the rear. "And to think I've been signing your praises. And look at poor Edgar. You've broken his heart."

They all stood on the stage for a full five minutes without saying a word.

The police had taken Clara Ashwood away. No one had words to express how they felt.

Edgar stood staring into space, Millicent by his side offering what comfort she could.

Evie forced herself to snap out of it. "Toodles, you should sit down."

"I'm feeling too edgy to do that, Birdie. Where's that butler of yours. Ah, there he is but there's no point in asking him for a drink. He looks like he needs one himself."

Toodles crossed the stage, poured a glass of champagne and handed it to Edgar. Patting her silk handbag, she said, "Let me know if you need something stronger." As an afterthought, she removed the flask and took a swig.

One by one, everyone began murmuring.

Henrietta found her voice. "Evangeline. What just happened?"

"Clara Ashwood failed to give the performance of her life. Just when she most needed to." Evie believed she might have been able to pull it off, if only she hadn't panicked.

Tom handed Evie a glass of champagne. As he lifted his own glass to his lips, he whispered, "What if she had an accomplice?"

"I'm sure Clara will use that as a bargaining chip."

The detective walked into the auditorium and made his way to the stage. "Well done, my lady."

"Me? Well done you. How did you find out the perfume bottle contained wood alcohol? I thought we'd have to wait until tomorrow for confirmation."

The detective smiled. "That American chemist I mentioned a while back, Dr. Gettler, devised a method for inspectors out on the field looking for the illegal substance. You heat a copper coil to red hot and plunge the metal into the substance in question. If wood alcohol is present, a small amount of formaldehyde is released. One whiff and your sense of smell is numbed."

"Heavens. Are you all right?"

He smiled. "Oh, yes." He dug inside his coat pocket and produced a small copper coil. "Truth is, I didn't get around to performing the test."

"You duped her into giving herself away?"

"I must admit, I took a gamble. There's a first time for everything. When I found the flask, I realized Clara Ashwood could claim it had been contaminated by the killer."

"The Countess entertained the same thought," Tom offered.

"Milady, you should take a bow," Caro said.

"I will do no such thing, Caro. You seem to forget," Evie grinned, "I have been presented."

EPILOGUE

Caro walked into Evie's bedroom and set a tray down. "I'm surprised at you, milady. Everyone is expecting you down for breakfast and here you are, still in bed."

"I'm in the process of getting up. I'll have a cup of coffee and then join the others. I have a busy day ahead of me and… in all honesty, I no longer wish to talk about Clara Ashwood. We all stayed up half the night talking of nothing… no one else."

"I seem to remember a lot of talk about you, milady."

"That was all nonsense. I do wish everyone would stop talking about my detecting skills and how I should set up an agency."

"I think it would be a marvelous idea. I could help you. In fact, I believe everyone expressed a desire to assist you."

"Well, I'm sorry but you will all be disappointed. Please start packing. We must head back to Halton House as soon as possible. I fear if we stay here any longer, Toodles and her co-conspirators will start looking around for a suitable office. I wouldn't be surprised if she has already designed the calling cards."

"With that attitude, you shouldn't be surprised if I take up her offer to go to America with her."

"You wouldn't…"

"Then again, if I had a reason to stay…"

"Are you blackmailing me? Wait a minute… You're giving me an ultimatum."

Caro shrugged. "Just think, if I left, you'd be stuck with Millicent. Or have you forgotten there's a lady's maid shortage?"

Evie grumbled under her breath. "Please tell me they're not really still talking about last night."

"Oh, yes. Especially now that the detective has his confession."

"He has? How do you know?"

"He's downstairs having breakfast. He arrived a few minutes ago to give you the news."

"Did she confess to hacking my roses?"

Caro's eyebrows curved up in surprise. "As a matter of fact, she did. She thought she was being very smart. But I'm surprised at you, milady. Surely, you are more interested in her other confession."

"Yes, of course. Did he say how Clara Ashwood managed to poison Horace's whisky?"

Caro nodded. "Apparently, one of his detectives figured it out even before she confessed. He compared Mr. Gibbins' appointment book entries to the whisky journal he kept recording which whisky he drank. The days he met with Clara Ashwood, he always drank from a particular bottle, one she gave him."

"But… But how did she get the methyl into the bottle?"

"She always claimed she wanted to test the whisky before giving it to him. So the bottles were always uncorked. As in, they were already poisoned."

"Did she give a reason? Surely it couldn't be about jealousy?"

"Oh, yes. Horace Gibbins felt the theater needed some fresh talent."

"That's it?"

"That's all it took for Clara Ashwood to devise a plan to get rid of him."

"And did the perfume have wood alcohol?"

"Yes, indeed. Quite a lot of it, enough to give her headaches and feelings of nausea."

Shaking her head, Evie drank her coffee. "Honestly, I will never understand people who are driven to take such extreme measures. And as for you going to America with Toodles... Well, you can just forget about it. You are staying here with me."

"Is this where you offer me an incentive?" Caro asked.

"I'm sure I can scrounge up another murder to keep you entertained."

"Really? But that would be marvelous."

Evie flung the bed covers off. "As I said, I have a busy day ahead."

"Busy day?"

"Yes." Evie brightened and grinned. "Here's another reason for you to stay on."

"What is it?"

"As long as we're in town, I thought I might take the opportunity and get an early start on my Christmas shopping. Seth is coming to stay with us at Halton House."

"Seth! Seth! Oh… When were you going to tell me?" Caro set the dress down and headed for the door.

"Where are you going? I haven't dressed yet."

"I'm sure you can manage by yourself. I need to tell the others, of course. We're going to have such a wonderful Christmas. Think of all the fun and games we'll have…"

"With the seven-year-old Earl of Woodridge? Games? What sort of games?"

"Milady, anyone would think you'd never had a childhood."

Clearly, she hadn't thought this through, but at least she'd managed to distract Caro from any more thoughts about setting up a lady's detective agency or going back to America with Toodles…

As for entertaining Caro with another murder…

I hope you've enjoyed reading Murder in the Third Act. I had a lot of fun writing it! Next in the Series: Murder and a Christmas Tree.

CPSIA information can be obtained
at www.ICGtesting.com
Printed in the USA
LVHW090036140420
653355LV00004B/1445